EDITORS
Susan Burmeister-Brown
Linda Burmeister Davies

CONSULTING EDITORS
Allyson Bourke
Brittney Corrigan-McElroy
Jennifer Jackson Reynolds
Roz Wais
Kris Wood

COPY EDITOR
Scott Allie

PROOFREADER
Rachel Penn

TYPESETTING & LAYOUT
Paul Morris

COVER ARTIST
Jane Zwinger

STORY ILLUSTRATOR
Jon Leon

PUBLISHED QUARTERLY
in spring, summer, fall, and winter by
Glimmer Train Press, Inc.
710 SW Madison Street, Suite 504, Portland, Oregon 97205-2900
Telephone: 503/221-0836   Facsimile: 503/221-0837
www.glimmertrain.com

PRINTED IN U.S.A.
Indexed in *The American Humanities Index.*

Glimmer Train (ISSN #1055-7520), registered in U.S. Patent and Trademark Office, is published quarterly, $32 per year in the U.S., by Glimmer Train Press, Inc., Suite 504, 710 SW Madison, Portland, OR 97205. Periodicals postage paid at Portland, OR, and additional mailing offices. POSTMASTER: Send address changes to Glimmer Train Press, Inc., Suite 504, 710 SW Madison, Portland, OR 97205.

ISSN # 1055-7520, ISBN # 1-880966-30-1, CPDA BIPAD # 79021

DISTRIBUTION: Bookstores can purchase *Glimmer Train Stories* through these distributors:
Anderson News Co., 6016 Brookvale Ln., #151, Knoxville, TN 37919
Ingram Periodicals, 1226 Heil Quaker Blvd., LaVergne, TN 37086
IPD, 674 Via de la Valle, #204, Solana Beach, CA 92075
Peribo PTY Ltd., 58 Beaumont Rd., Mt. Kuring-Gai, NSW 2080, AUSTRALIA
Ubiquity, 607 Degraw St., Brooklyn, NY 11217

SUBSCRIPTION SVCS: EBSCO, Faxon, READMORE, TURNER SUBSCRIPTIONS, BLACKWELL'S UK

Subscription rates: One year, $32 within the U.S. (Visa/MC/check). Airmail to Canada, $43; outside North America, $54. Payable by Visa/MC or check for U.S. dollars drawn on a U.S. bank.

Attention short-story writers: We pay $500 for first publication and onetime anthology rights. Please include a self-addressed, sufficiently stamped envelope with your submission. Send manuscripts in January, April, July, and October. Send SASE for guidelines, or visit our website for information on our Short-Story Award for New Writers, our Very Short Fiction Award, and our Fiction and Poetry Opens.

Glimmer Train Press also offers **Writers Ask**—*nuts, bolts, and informed perspectives—a quarterly newsletter for the committed writer. One year, four issues, $20 within the U.S. ($26 beyond the U.S.), Visa, MC or check to Glimmer Train Press, Inc., or order online at www.glimmertrain.com.*

Dedication

Andre Dubus was a champion
of the short story and of the
short-story writer. Generous,
forthright, and fearless—
he will be sorely missed.

Andre Dubus
Born 1936
Died 1999

CONTENTS

ONTENTS

Monica Wood

Here I am, in my aunt's garden. I did have clothes;
apparently I chose not to wear them.

Monica Wood is the author of *Secret Language*, a novel; *Description*, a book on fiction writing; and three educational books on teaching contemporary literature. Her short stories have been widely published and anthologized, most recently in *Glimmer Train*, *Redbook*, *Tampa Review*, and *Best American Mystery Stories 1997*. "Ernie's Ark," which appeared in *Glimmer Train*, won a 1998 Pushcart Prize.

MONICA WOOD
Frost: A Love Story

*T*he little girl's mother died coming home one night from the public library where she worked shelving both rare and ordinary books, a job ideal for a woman of her limited education and limitless imagination. It was her job, also, to lock up, which she did that night, certain of the evening ahead of her, her children asleep in their beds, her husband slumbering in a chair, waiting. The keys plinked against her palm in the cool, misty air. Her high heels clicked over the granite steps and across the pavement. Then, the gentle churring of her car engine, a crackle from the radio, the end-of-day sounds to which she had become happily accustomed. Halfway home, the driver of a Volkswagen Beetle jumped the guardrail on Route 4 and hurtled clean across the waxed hood of the little girl's mother's brand-new Pontiac station wagon, which slipped off the glassy road in a long, religious silence, until it crumpled into the trees.

In an era when parents piled kids into the back like a load of Christmas presents, the station wagon held little in the way of safety features. But because the little girl's mother made grand, motherly efforts to be practical in ways that belied her fluttery beauty and love of dancing, the new station wagon did harbor early-edition safety restraints, including a lap belt in the driver's seat, which on the night in question had been buckled and tightened, judging from the pelvic bruising. Upon impact, the belt came apart. Or she unbuckled herself out of shock. Or (this is what the little girl thought) an angel wafted down and removed the restraint from a woman who no longer required restraining. This last was the little girl's regret, for she dearly wanted her mother fastened to the earth.

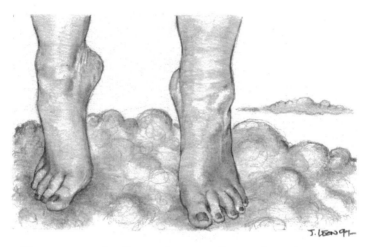

The new car also featured an excellent radio, which, as the story goes, was still playing the country countdown when they found the library assistant's body lying calmly across the vinyl expanse of the front seat. Her face was smooth as beach stone, her grey dress draped modestly below the knees, her thin calves lying side by side. Her feet were perched together, the toenails painted "Kiss Me" red and pointed precisely downward from her broken ankles as if she might be making ready to present a difficult dance step.

Which is how the little girl, at the age of eight, hearing this whispered version of her mother's death from witnesses she did not know, had to imagine her mother ever after: in heaven with her bare calves showing, standing on tippy toe, teaching something complicated to God.

The little girl's father was a weak man who fell vague and drowsy after the death of his wife. Late that winter, he left a cigarette burning in an armchair. And another on the couch. And another in an ashtray on a window sill under a polyester curtain. Nothing back then was flameproof, including the one-piece pajamas favored by the little girl's baby brothers. She was sleeping at a friend's that night, her first sleepover, her first entry into a world of women since her mother's abrupt departure. When the friend's mother woke her the next morning she chose her words gently, and the little girl pictured a pinkish curl of smoke carrying the babies' souls straight to the cold, unblinking heavens. Her father, his face as pale as her mother's headstone, spoke of life's unfathomable cycle, then wandered away. The little girl understood, at the age of eight, not only that her loved ones had left her for good, but that anyone who came near her would, sooner or later (more likely sooner, given her unlucky history), fade utterly from the earth's shuddery crust.

This is a truth we all face. Though not at eight.

The little girl grew up to reject a long line of feverish suitors, for she inherited her mother's graceful lines and smooth skin and dancer's legs. She rejected one crimson-faced boy after another—even the ones she liked, even the ones who stirred her toes (which she painted, always, in her mother's honor). She kept no pets, although it occurred to her briefly—on the occasion of her graduation from college, when she left the dais after her valedictory to an empty swatch of grass in which a beaming relative, had she had one, might have stood to congratulate her—that she might consider a notoriously long-lived pet, a horse or parrot or monkey. But the moment passed as she removed her mortar board and skipped the luncheon, and went to clean out her dormitory room, a single.

She went to another school for four more years to study fossils. Turning the dry pages of dry, old books in the light of one library or another, she was reminded again and again of her mother. She imagined that last night, the keys to the library doors jangling against her mother's translucent palm, the tippy-tapping walk out to the brand-new station wagon, the opening of the car door, the useless click of the lap belt, the crackle of the radio, the turning engine. Whether her mother kicked off her shoes right then, grabbing the gas pedal with her pretty toes, or whether her shoes came off during the crash, she did not know, but she liked to think of her mother driving barefoot in autumn, her feet the most heedless part of her, the narrow toes keeping time. She imagined, too, a melodious thrumming emanating from her mother's lips as she hummed along with Charley Pride or Tammy Wynette. This was her one comfort, the thought of her mother's humming and tapping, that simple sign of contentment accompanying her sudden, spectacular, unwanted end.

If the little girl, now a woman, could be said to love anything living, it would be the flower garden she maintained in her tiny front yard. Her house was tiny, too, and covered with blue shingles, a few convenient miles from the lab where she worked sorting bones. The garden was too modest to be a showpiece, but people in the neighborhood noticed it anyway, for she had some interesting plants nestled among the usual coreopsis and shasta daisies, including an out-of-zone hibiscus with big, red, shameless, trumpet-shaped flowers. Long before first frost in autumn, she would bury her garden in leaves, cutting back even the plants that had not finished blooming, her heart heavy with ritual and a vague sadness and a premature aching for spring.

Her last act every summer was to dig up the hibiscus and bring it inside where it resided in a planter in the foyer of her house. Each spring she unearthed it again and placed it in the same spot at the center of her garden. The plant had been brought over by a young man from the lab who thought a houseplant might please his taciturn, cheerless, beautiful colleague. It might even inspire her to accept his offer of dinner someplace, a cup of coffee, a movie maybe; which— needless to say, since the fellow was exactly her age with the male animal's disadvantage in life span—it did not. Still, the plant pleased her, and the effort. The image of her gift-bearing colleague's thin, hairy arms encircling the plant as he loped up her walk became as fixed in her memory as her mother's painted toes poised for dancing. She liked his gold-red hair, his greenish eyes, his long fingers, and his name: Jarrod. She continued to think of him even after he left the lab and went to work at the main campus; her memory had plenty of room, as she had collected so few experiences since those early, indelible ones. She filled it with thoughts of Jarrod, about whom she knew next to nothing. She considered him a friend.

Then came a spring like no other, a sunny, ripe March, crocuses popping through snowmelt like good news, tulips opening before tax day, a bewildering act of God that had the little girl, now a woman, furtively checking the sky for signs of the people she'd lost. She saw clouds shaped like her mother's ankles, her baby brothers' ears, her father's sloped, unhappy shoulders. One day after another she saw sun, benign white gusts of clouds, then more sun, then a gentle, restorative rain, tuffets of snow vanishing like light, temperatures above sixty. In her one act of faith since the death of her mother, she brought out the hibiscus, by now a heavy, bushy ornament, and dragged it down over her front steps in a struggle so mighty it induced little yips of effort from her throat. As was her custom, she spent the entire afternoon unearthing the thing from its winter grave and returning it to its rightful place in the earth. She laughed. She thought of Jarrod and his thin arms.

But this was April. This was New England. In two days or three, after an inevitable frost turned her ornament of faith into a thicket of broken sticks, she flung open her door at six in the morning, barefoot, barely dressed, thudding down the cold steps, her high, still-girlish voice keening far into the neighbors' windows. She bent her body over the dead thing, its stiff branches pressing at tender spots on her skin. She got up and flailed her arms, turned her throat to the sky, opened her mouth wide, made sounds that lifted birds from the trees.

The woman across the street looked out at the flying hair, the waving arms. She murmured, half-standing, to her husband, "Will you look at that," and to her five-year-old son, "Don't look at that." The husband, who like the other neighbors considered the young woman in the shingled house a cold fish in a lab coat, thought of a scene in a cheap movie where the grips or best boys or what have you keep spraying the heroine's face with a mister between takes. He squinted over his paper at the unbuckled despair in the odd little garden and wondered when in his life, if ever, he would see again a spectacle such as this. He looked away, embarrassed, then looked out again.

She began to whirl, her toes tearing into the damp, half-frozen earth. More neighbors, some of whom did not know each other and none of whom knew the young woman, gaped from their doorways. She danced around the broken thing, cursing the sky, as if her useless cawing might wake the dead plant, restore its waxy leaves, sprout the red, swollen buds that opened every August. When finally she turned her face from the clouds, she raced up the steps for her car keys, hauled a coat over her shoulders, left the door of her house hanging open like a surprised face, and, still barefoot, got into her car to find the man who had given her the plant. Jarrod. It had been four years. She resolved to find him inside the campus research center, a maze of white, conical buildings stacked one upon the other. The entrances were legion, requiring card keys and polite conversations with bored watchmen. She had inherited her mother's practical nature, and also, as it turned out, her swift-moving feet; within an hour she found him. Staring into his startled, marvelling face, she told him what had become of the plant, describing in a fountain of words its emerging beauty, its seasonal trips to and from her garden, its final surrender to her foolish impulse. Then she stopped. Her feet were still, her head slightly tilted, her hands clasped in a perfect calm.

It was he who ran out of breath: his color rose, his mouth parted in a stupid, grateful wonderment. She stood before him, her own color blazing, her hair sprawled over her shoulders, bright spots of nail polish glinting through the dirt that covered her feet. She lifted one foot, then the other, visited by a curious thrumming that could be no other thing than her mother's spirit coursing through her. Closing her eyes, she welcomed her mother back, apologized for believing the dead stay dead. Her lips began to move. She spoke his name: Jarrod. Again she said it, liking the sound. It was heavy with consonants, rooted, earthbound. She asked him to replace what he had given her, to appear on her walk one more time, to bestow upon her one more chance, his arms circled around something absolutely alive.

George Stolz

Strange as it may seem, I possess no photos of myself as a child, nor can I get my hands on any. I do, however, happen to have a photo that I took as a child—this photo, of the rest of my family (only my sister is missing). It was taken in Pennsylvania, in the mountains, on the day of a full solar eclipse. And since it is the family that instills in us the harsh yet porous edge between everything we are and everything we are not, I might go so far as to say that I too am outlined somewhere in this composition.

George Stolz was born in New York City and grew up in Pennsylvania. He attended Columbia College and now lives in Madrid, where he writes frequently about art. He is currently at work on a novel.

GEORGE STOLZ
The Boy Who Lay Down

*E*arly on a Saturday evening in the kitchen of a small New York City apartment a young man named Gene tilted a tarnished teakettle and splashed scalding water into a yellowed ceramic teacup. A telephone was wedged in the crook between his shoulder and neck as he limped about the room fixing the tea; finishing the preparations, he crossed to the cupboard and drew down a battered hip flask, half-filled with brandy. He added a measure of its contents to the quickly coloring water, restoppered the flask, and replaced it on the shelf. He set the cup on the table and allowed the two old teabags in it to steep, setting himself down in one of the kitchen's mismatched metal folding chairs, watching and stirring. With the telephone still pressed tight against his ear, he leaned backward in the chair and looked across the room, out through the glass of its single curtainless window. He saw in the darkness that snow still slowly fell. Despite the streaming sound of the female voice pouring from the telephone into his ear he noticed, in the sonal wake left behind the now-vanished scream of the tea-kettle's whistling, a peculiar silence of which on this night he seemed the center: the evening silence of his neighborhood, the silence of the muffling nighttime snow, the silence of his home. He tried to sip silently as she continued.

"Last night I wanted to go to Miami and none of my cousins would take me. We just went out around here instead. We went to about four different places and I hated all of them. Everyone got drunk, even Sheila. She came with us dancing, can you believe it? But she didn't dance, of course. She was drunk. You should have seen David, it was so funny. He was calling everybody stupid and then he passed out and they had to carry him out to his car and drive him home.

"Babe, I miss you. I'll see you Monday, right?"

Outside Gene's kitchen window the blue-white descending curtain of falling snow gleamed coolly in the night and piled gently on the nearby low-lying rooves. Gene watched while carefully savoring the complementary sensations that composed the hot, spiked tea: he didn't answer her question. She continued.

"I'm so hungry. I haven't eaten all day. I don't want to spend the whole time down here in my brother's little house in his little town. I want to go to Miami. They told me it's only a half-hour drive away from here. Honey, when are you going to teach me how to drive? I want to go to Miami in the morning. I want to look at all that architecture, do some shopping, then go to the beach in the afternoon and have a nice dinner after. Lobster. I'm so bored. I really hate this. I knew I shouldn't have let you let me come here without you. What are you doing, anyway?"

"Nothing. I'm just resting my ankle," Gene finally answered. "I've been watching it snow."

"It's snowing in New York! Now I bet you're sorry you didn't come, aren't you? Is it cold? I guess it must be, if it's snowing. Gene, promise me you won't go out with your ankle like that and slip on the ice. It's snowing in New York! Now I'm glad I came. But, babe, I'm so hungry. I haven't eaten all day. Hold on a minute, let me see what they're cooking."

Gene heard through the telephone the snap of her quick footsteps and then heard her faraway voice announce in triumph that it was snowing in New York. The announcement was followed by a cheer of spitefully delighted voices. Outside his window a heavy thudding sound, as of something having fallen, startled him. He twisted toward the window; peering through the falling snow, he thought he glimpsed a dark form moving quickly across the roof of the lower neighboring building. He leaned forward, focusing, but could make out nothing. His girlfriend's voice returned.

"Babe, let me let you go now. I'm going to eat what they're cooking for dinner. But I miss you. I'll see you Monday, right? Monday night? Tell me I will, please tell me I will. My plane gets in at 8:30."

"Don't worry, I'll be here," he answered. "I'm not going anywhere."

"Thank you, honey. Now let me let you go. Love you."

He was about to hang up the telephone when he heard her voice, tiny and metallic, calling frantically through the black plastic telephone still in his hand.

"Babe, babe, babe, babe, babe! Are you there?"

"I'm here."

"Babe, make the snow melt by Monday, okay?"

Gene returned the receiver to its cradle and as the warmth and mixed flavors of the tea comforted his hands and head, he closed his eyes and tried to imagine the wedding of his girlfriend's cousin. He tried but failed: Florida was too far away, the unslanting intensity of its midday light too strong and shadowless, its colors too simple and bright. Winter weddings were all he could see: early darkness and windows opaque with steam, blasts of frigid air at every opening of a door, guests bundled in furs and heavy coats, chandeliers of sparkling yellow light overhead, and wineglasses glittering like rubies below. The bride was always haggard, her face drawn and shadow ridden, her eyes wandering and distracted. The groom was always flushed and looking as if he were wearing a secret girdle that was bound too tightly, his voice high and sharp with nerves.

He remembered a snowy wedding held north of the city in what had once been the grand estate of an industrial baron. Both a rabbi and a Protestant minister consecrated the union with alternating sets of wedding vows. The parents of the indecisive and twice-joined couple, awed by their children's ingenuity in resolving the conflict of their nagging, residual faiths, enthusiastically advocated the same solution to all the other parents of as-yet-unmarried children. Gene slipped away unnoticed from the wedding's reception as soon as he heard the hired band begin tuning their instruments, escaping the inevitable dancing by going up the wide stairs that led from the ballroom to the rented mansion's peaceful upper floors. He padded at his leisure along thick dark carpets, running his hand along polished mahogany, and looking in over the cordons of velvet that drooped across the rooms' thresholds, barring entrance. He came to a stop at the central corridor's end in front of a large, beveled-glass window that revealed the grandeur of the grounds behind the estate. Standing in front of the window, wineglass in hand, and hearing only the faintest strains of the wedding band's tinny music, he saw outside in the silent night two parallel rows of trees, planted in perfect symmetry, filing across the yard away from the mansion. At the far end of the rows of trees stood a single evergreen towering over the rest, its conical shape dressed from head to foot in a pure white gown of moist snow that glittered like rhinestones or even stars: a strong, proud, and peaceful bride poised in the moonlit darkness.

He opened his eyes to the blue fluorescent light of the kitchen and, reverie breaking, rose from the chair and crossed the room toward the window in front of him. He looked down into the darkness for traces of what he had thought was someone running across the low flat rooftop of the neighboring building. It was covered to a uniform thickness by new and unruffled snow, crisscrossed only by the night-time shadows of the sloppily strung laundry lines and television cable wires hanging overhead. The rooftop was closed off on all sides, shielded from the street by the taller front part of the building, while the far end abutted the rear wall of a synagogue. The painted bricks of the synagogue's high white wall were as smooth and unmarked as the surface of the snow, except for one round, ocular formation of stained glass centered in the wall's upper reaches.

Gene placed his palms on the window's wide sill and looked out, remembering a poem that had been used as the text for a short, spare piece for solo male dancer, a piece that he had once performed. The central image of the poem still lingered in his memory: an image in which a busy city street, forced into silence and calm by a sudden heavy snowfall, was likened to an agnostic removing his hat and bowing his head upon entering a church. It was an image he had not liked. It had seemed ungraceful and pedestrian and difficult to dance to, but at the same time had confused him and in confusing him had followed him through the years and into every city snow-fall. Snow still did not seem spiritual to him. It was neither purging nor cleansing, neither vengeful and victorious nor baptismal and redemptive, neither fire nor rain. He looked up at the darkened, hovering eye of the synagogue, trying to make out the patterns hidden within the soot-covered stained glass, when he saw out of the corner of his eye, behind the glass of the window in the apartment next to his, the face of a man staring wild-eyed at the snow.

The man wore no shirt: his shining white flesh reflected the incoming light in the otherwise darkened window. A wide belt barely held up a pair of baggy trousers on his scrawny body. He stood in a dark room holding a whiskless broomstick in one hand. Gene could hear nothing across the distance and through the two panes of glass that separated them, but he could see by the light shining in that the man was screaming, his mouth moving rapidly, his face contorted. Gene recognized the man as the nephew of Señora Mercedes García, the elderly Cuban woman who was his neighbor. Gene stared, transfixed by the luminescent apparition, watching as the nephew's agitation increased. When the nephew suddenly threw open the window and leaned out, screaming, Gene at the same moment jumped backward involuntarily, knocking the teacup off the sill and onto the floor where it smashed, scattering tea-stained slivers and shards in an amber puddle. Gene stood sideways beside the window, holding his body rigid and out of sight of Señora García's nephew.

"Come on, you motherless fuckers!" the nephew screamed in a high, choked rasp. "Come on! Come on! I'll kill you mothers!"

The nephew began pointing the broomstick as if it were a rifle, aiming and firing erratically at some invisible target in the snow with one arm while the other arm flailed uncontrollably at his side. His head shook as if palsied. He jerked the broomstick up over his head and, without noticing, knocked from the windowsill one of his aunt's large earthen planters, full of fallow dirt. A moment later the planter landed with a snow-muffled crash. At the sound of the planter's impact the nephew stopped screaming and stopped moving. He stood paralyzed, a chiaroscuro portrait framed in the window, and Gene saw clearly for one moment that terror filled his eyes, making them dance. Gene also saw beads of sweat on his face and chest, despite the freezing air. The nephew broke his pose and stepped back quickly, pulling down the window sash hard, and withdrew into the unlighted rooms of Señora García's apartment.

20

With the closing of the window Gene realized that he too was terrified. His breathing had become short and he had not swallowed since first seeing the nephew. In jumping backward he had jarred his injured ankle, and in knocking over the teacup he had bruised the small bones in the back of his hand. He sat down on the floor, shaken, and tried to gather his wits. He picked up the pieces of the broken teacup and swabbed the floor with a white rag, losing himself in thoughts of Señora García and her nephew. Though they had been neighbors for years, he knew little about her other than that she was a small grey woman who worked in a hospital and who, with the exception of her nephew's visits, seemed to live utterly alone. Gene had watched her returning from work, hastily unlocking the tenement's street door and pressing it closed with her back, and resting there for a moment as she trembled with the fear born of walking New York City's streets, a daily fear among the elderly. She had once surprised Gene by telling him, as they stood chatting in the hallway onto which both their apartment doors opened, that as a young girl many years before she used to accompany her father in the streets and cabarets of la Habana, playing the guitar while he played the cuatro and sang. Gene found the scene difficult to picture, and in straining to do so he stared at her so hard that she sensed his incredulity. Trying to convince him, she abruptly launched into a pantomime of herself performing. Her eyes widened and her face lit up in a frozen, harlequin-like rictus while she held an invisible guitar high in the Cuban style, strumming the air with splayed fingers. But even then the greyness enshrouding her did not disperse. She told Gene that she had sold the guitar, years ago, for much money.

"Oh yes," she had said, nodding her head, "I used to play beautifully."

Gene wondered where Señora García might be on a Saturday night. She was not much older than his own mother, who also lived very much alone but who was not yet powdered with the heavy grey dust of age. His mother was slender and energetic, her once naturally blond hair now artificially so, but an undiminished blue still blazing in her eyes with a pride and vanity that had been only toughened by the inevitable battering of the years. It was from his mother that Gene had learned to drink tea, although his own tastes never approached the range and cultivation of hers. She collected teas, fennels and cinnamons, gingers and jasmines, chamomiles, chrysanthemums and sasparillas, storing them in glass jars with tightly screwed-on metal lids, steeping an ever-changing variety of blends while tending the shop that catered expertly to the frivolous tastes of tourists. She carefully packed pouches to accompany her on long winter ski vacations, and on solitary nights she sipped delicately while sitting in one of her green wingback chairs by the yellow light of one of her precious antique lamps, reading the memoirs of famous figures from history. Gene was her only child—the complications of his birth had seen to that, as well as having contributed to his father's flight, as she often told him when he was young and receiving one of her severe beatings.

"Your name is Eugene," he could still hear her saying, "and Eugene means well bred. Don't ever forget that."

Gene's thoughts of Señora García and his mother led him to realize that he knew virtually nothing about Señora García's nephew. In their brief exchanges in the building's doorway and corridors, both Gene and the nephew were quiet and always polite, never exchanging more words than a passing hello, but the nephew's deep-seated unhappiness had always been visible in the pained attempts at smiles of salutation that threatened to shatter his acne-scarred, strong-boned face. Gene struggled to reconcile the memory of that quiet man, in age and bearing much resembling Gene himself, with the nightmare vision of the rage-filled face in the window, which

had not ceased stirring up in Gene directionless and dispro-
portionate sensations of dread. Gene felt he could not move.
He dared not cross in front of the window, not even to fix
another cup of tea, for fear of what he might see in that other
window which obliquely mirrored his own; yet the wall
against which his back was pressed as he sat on the floor and
which separated the two apartments seemed to have grown
thinner, to have acquired the thinness of a membrane, threat-
ening osmosis. Gene was on the verge of rising to reach for his
brandy flask when a short series of sharp raps on the
apartment's metal front door nearly stopped his heart, forcing
the air from his lungs in a guttural gasp. He stood at once,
dropping the white rag, but upon standing stumbled on his
weak ankle. As he staggered toward the front door he reached
for the crutch that was propped upright in the apartment's
foyer. The quick, hard raps were repeated.

"Who is it?" Gene called out through the closed door. His
mouth was dry. He was answered by a female voice too loud
for the size and acoustics of the tenement's hallway.

"It's the police. Please open the door."

Gene leaned on his crutch and opened the door slightly,
and saw two police officers, a woman and a man, in the dim
light of the hallway. The shapelessness of their thick and
heavy outergarments did not hide the bulging lines of their
awkward bulletproof vests, and at the sight of the two
holstered revolvers dangling from their waists Gene felt a
wave of nausea.

"Can we speak to you for a moment?" the policewoman
asked through the narrow opening. The policeman, as if it
were his custom, stood silently behind her, watching Gene.

"Of course," Gene said, suddenly desiring to tell them
everything, to unburden his heart to the comfort and security
of authority. He wanted to tell them of poor Señora García
and her crazed nephew, and as well of his own terror and

solitude on a Saturday night, breaking a yellowed teacup and sitting on the floor, not knowing what to do, and thinking about his mother instead. He unfastened the chain and opened the door wide, moving to usher the police officers into his apartment, when he saw that the police officers were not alone, that Señora García's nephew was with them in the hallway, standing to the side where Gene, peering out from within the apartment, had not before been able to see him. Gene wished mightily that he had not opened the door, but knew that he could not, as he was tempted, slam it closed now.

"Have you seen anyone behind the building tonight, trying to break in?" the policewoman asked. The overhead fluorescent light reflected off the taut brown skin of her curved cheeks in distorted rectangular patches as she fixed her inexpressive eyes on Gene.

The collision between his desire to tell the police all and his horror at feeling the gaze of Señora García's nephew prevented Gene from responding. He grimaced and took one step backward into his apartment, just out of the nephew's field of vision. Looking straight at the policewoman he raised and lowered his eyebrows while jerking his head toward the nephew, trying to communicate through his fluttering facial contortions that she must get rid of the madman before he could answer her question. She stared at Gene as if he and not the nephew were mad. Finally the policeman, impatient, spoke to Gene.

"He says some kids were trying to get in back there to attack him," the policeman said, angling his thumb toward Señora García's nephew. "Did you see anything? He says they had a gun."

Señora García's nephew stepped sideways into the doorway and watched Gene over the policewoman's big blue shoulder. His face was more gaunt than ever. The veins running along either side of his neck bulged. His eyes both glared and implored while he blinked ferociously.

"I've seen them out there before," Gene answered, looking back and forth between the suddenly distant faces of the two police officers and avoiding the nephew's eyes. "I haven't seen them tonight, but I wasn't really looking. But I have seen them before. They play out there, on the next roof. A bunch of neighborhood kids."

"Did you see a gun?" the policeman pressed Gene.

"I told you, I didn't even see them tonight," Gene said, shrugging his shoulders.

"All right, all right, I gotcha," the policewoman said with finality. She turned from Gene and began conferring with her partner, their mumbling voices too low for Gene to decipher.

"Okay now? Is that it?" Gene interrupted them.

"Yeah, okay. Thanks," the policewoman said without turning back to look at Gene.

Gene closed the door before his eyes met those of Señora García's nephew again. In his haste to answer the door he had not turned on the foyer's overhead light, so that with the closing of the door he stood leaning on the crutch in near-darkness, catching his breath. His ankle throbbed. He cupped his ear to the door, still hoping with frantic desperation that the police officers might do something to help him. He heard two sets of clunky departing footsteps walk the length of the hallway and descend the stairs and he caught the echo in the stairwell of their loud, static-filled police radio just before the door to the street below crashed closed. He waited with his ear to the metal, hearing only his own hard breathing, but listening for that other sound, the sound of the door to Señora García's apartment falling shut. That sound did not come. In its stead Gene heard the sound of a hand fumbling with the unwieldy machinery of the mechanical doorbell of his own door. He closed his eyes, inhaled through his nose, and swallowed forcefully, trying to compose himself, to turn his mind into a single sheet of stark, blank white paper as he had once been taught to do when struggling with stage fright. He swung the door open before the doorbell had sounded.

Señora García's nephew raised his head to look up at Gene in the doorway while his hand continued groping for the doorbell a moment longer, as if his addled brain had been unable to halt one movement of his body before beginning another. Gene anchored the crutch's rubber tip and stepped forward, meeting the nephew squarely in the threshold, a distance of inches separating the two men. Gene felt the nephew's warm breath on his neck and involuntarily held his own, as if threatened with contagion of the other's madness.

"So you did see 'em, right?" the nephew asked. "You saw 'em out there?"

The nephew's eyes were fixed on Gene's even while his head turned slowly and minutely from side to side. His loose jaw continued moving after he had finished speaking, as if chewing cud, and the corners of his purple-lipped mouth jumped spastically, as if tugged by the strings of some cruel puppeteer. Gene saw clearly that the nephew was cocaine-mad, a crackhead gone to pieces.

"They're just kids out there, they're just playing," Gene said.

"Oh, no, man, you're fucked up if that's what you think. They have a gun, I'm telling you. They're not playing." The embers of the nephew's mad terror suddenly flared, fanned by Gene's doubt and fueled by his own urgent certainty. His voice leapt to a scream's pitch. "They're right out *there!*"

The nephew abruptly swung the broomstick in order to point at the back of the building, and in so doing struck Gene's crutch, knocking it sideways and jarring Gene loose. Gene fell forward, seeing in a flash nothing but the intricate patterns of the filthy, black-and-white-tiled floor. With one quick, trained hand he caught himself mid-fall on the crutch, while the other hand, having reflexively reached out toward the floor in order to break his fall, landed lightly, bearing no weight, on the nephew's foot. The delicate and narrow feet were bare and dirty, and Gene, bowed down, at once sensed the extent of the nephew's frailty and fragility. Through his fingertips he felt the chill in the marble on which the nephew stood.

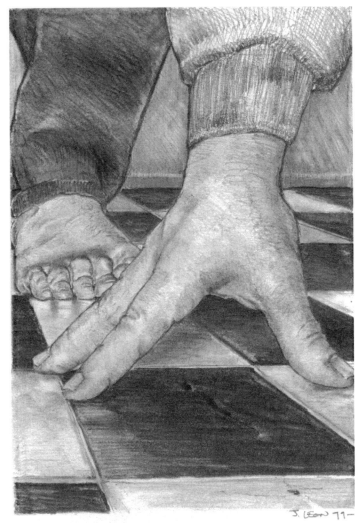

Gene raised himself upright, but the nephew still looked down to the spot where Gene had touched his bare flesh. The arm that held the broomstick hung limp at his side. Gene saw that he was shivering.

"They were trying to kill me," the nephew said in a low voice, knitting his thick black eyebrows. He looked up, his eyes pleading with Gene. "They were trying to kill me."

"So stay away from the window," Gene said.

Gene brushed off his palm on the side of his leg and stepped back into his apartment, turning his back on Señora García's nephew. He locked the door and crossed the darkened foyer into the light of the kitchen, and once again stood in front of the window, feeling the drafts of frigid air snaking around the loose panes of glass. He looked out past his own reflection, through the billowing mantle and down to the flickers of wettening snow that flashed incessantly on the eerie, isolated rooftop. He had often seen the neighborhood boys there, playing games with sticks and cans and rules too elaborate for Gene to understand from afar. As he thought of those groups of boys, memories of his own solitary boyhood returned: memories of bleak afternoons spent crossing the snow-covered fields of his New England home, fields utterly desolate save for the dried and crackling carcasses of cornstalk stumps marking their straight and narrow rows even in sleep and death; and memories of a cold so fierce that voices could not carry, not even the voice of the boy who shouted his own name as he ran alone in a wind so strong and loud that it seemed to be rushing from within his own head. He remembered himself again as the boy who lay down in the snow after an old man who lived nearby told him that snow could keep a body warm, that back when the country was in the Great Depression hoboes such as himself had survived the western winters by tunneling into the snow at night and packing it around them in icy shells that held their bodies' warmth while they slept, forgetful in their dreaming of their waking misery. That boy, practicing for the hobo life he hoped someday to lead, lay down in the snow; and afterward, scarred by the cold's sharpened blade, staggered home, unable to stop his sobbing.

Janet Desaulniers

*When I was three and four and five years old,
my mother and grandmother and great grandmother
believed I would enjoy modeling high-priced
children's fashions.*

Janet Desaulnier's fiction has appeared in the *New Yorker*, *Ploughshares*, *TriQuarterly*, the *New England Review*, and the *Pushcart Prize* anthology, among other publications. She directs the MFA in Writing program at The School of the Art Institute of Chicago and lives with her husband and son in Evanston, Illinois.

JANET DESAULNIERS
Mothers without Children

$\mathcal{J}$oy brings the meeting to order. A huge pious woman
who does not diet, she maintains she is happy the way she is.
Two hundred, thirty-six pounds, she says flatly, not prideful,
not rueful. Next to her, Charlene, a wraith with a frightened,
reedy voice many of us in the group find unnerving, as if
someone or something has squeezed her windpipe partially
shut, looks vaguely ashamed. It's difficult to know if she's
ashamed because Joy weighs 236 pounds or because Joy is
comfortable speaking facts.

Joy leads our prayer. She says, "Father, watch over our children. Forgive the men. Hold us from hatred. Help us to know
they've stolen our children, not our souls."

We all say amen, except Annalise. At Annalise's first meeting,
we noted her silence, and Joy explained to her that we did not
mean the opening prayer to offend, that of course different
people had different ideas of God. For some, he was the force
of creation; for others, a force inside themselves; for others, a
force inside the group. All that was fine with us, Joy said.

Annalise looked unaffected, which drew our curiosity. At
our first meetings most of us had been shy or tearful or
explosive, but Annalise maintained a brittle poise. She smoked
premium-length cigarettes, one after the other, drawing them

delicately from a hard leather case she wore clipped to the belt of her blue jeans.

"I believe in God," Annalise told Joy that night. "The same one you do. The one who sees all and hears all and does all. And I want him to know I'm angry, that he screwed up, that yes, yes, all of eternity without a mistake, but here it is. Me. This. You."

Tonight, as we wait for someone to begin, Annalise stares across the circle at Barbara, who shared with us last week that she had taken a lover, her first, who is a woman, also her first. Barbara worried about what she called "the drama" of such a choice. Hadn't there been enough drama in her life, she said, as if there were a limit on how much drama one life could contain. Tonight, under Annalise's attention, Barbara fidgets, moving her long feet, which she had tucked under her in the chair, back to the floor.

"You know, I've been mulling you over," Annalise says to her. "You and your new girlfriend. And I think you're soft-pedaling the issue. I want men to know that I reject them categorically. If I could, I'd wear a sign. And I want them to know it's not a matter of some erotic preference. It's just good judgment. They're killers."

Annalise has two boys, six and eight, missing for just over a year. Twice, on their birthdays, her husband has mailed her locks of their hair. About her own sons Annalise once said, "When I find them, I'll beat them bloody. I'll cook them for dinner. I'll devour them."

Tonight Joy smiles at her and says, "Anger is empowerment, too."

Irene, a tremulous woman, dainty and prim, with tiny hands and feet, nods first at Annalise, then at Barbara, then at Joy. Immediately the rest of us look at the floor. Irene was on a talk show last week, though we warned her against it. She was just a member of the audience, but they paid her plane fare out there to tell her story from the front row. Some of us got together to watch. When Irene's turn came to speak, she stood, swallowed, and nodded at the camera twice. Two thousand miles away, we sat frozen in our chairs as her eyes filled up. She just stood there.

Come on, Irene, we thought.

The host put his hand on her shoulder and lowered his eyes.

"My daughter," Irene said, quivering under his hand. She looked wildly around the studio and said it again. "My daughter." No more words came.

The host sat her down gently, looked at his feet a little longer, and went on.

Oh no, we thought. Irene.

It's her first meeting back, but so far no one has mentioned the show, our eyes flitting around the room, avoiding the subject in each other's faces. In the vicinity of Annalise, though, Irene stands suddenly and breaks for the door, her face puffy with emotion. Near the cookies and coffeepot, she turns back to us, throws her patent-leather pocketbook to the floor, and then slides down the wall, weeping.

"I couldn't even tell the story." She speaks between sobs. "My god, what if she saw me? What if she saw me like that?"

Joy picks up the pocketbook, tucks it under Irene's arm, and leads her out to the car. No one says anything. Annalise takes longer than is necessary to crush out her cigarette. This is self-help, Joy has told us before, but sometimes you have to lean.

A new girl, young, probably not yet thirty, but with strands of grey scattered through her long dark hair, begins to cry. She is pregnant, and we find this notable, unmentionable. Raising her face from her handkerchief, she tells us that her new husband feels she should try now to quiet her interest in the missing child. He has encouraged her to buy new curtains and bedding and baby clothes.

"It isn't that he says so," she tells us, "but in his silences, in his body as he makes love to me, I think he believes he should be powerful enough to obliterate what happened. 'It won't ever happen again' is what he says."

She buries her face in her handkerchief again, and we watch her shoulders heave. Then she raises her chin, looks solemnly at us. It hurts to look back at her. "He doesn't change *any-thing*" is what she says.

We look to each other, to the door, but Joy doesn't appear. Even Annalise is restive, struggling to open a new pack of cigarettes.

"You have to believe your child is alive and safe," Charlene says. "She's just somewhere else, sleeping and getting up in the morning and maybe going to school."

Annalise expels a stream of smoke. "How can you be so mild, Charlene? Get out of your chair, at least, if you mean to help someone. Are you afraid you'll muss your hair?" She turns to the new girl. "Listen, you look young enough to hunt him down, pull a trigger, and still survive the prison term."

We sit quietly then. It's possible that Joy drove Irene home. Perhaps that's why we think of Joy's story, and why we tell it to the new one, as if it were our story or her story and in it were form, the bare scaffolding of meaning, the answer she's asking for.

After Joy's husband took her three boys and all their money, she sold what he'd left behind, bought a van, and went after him. For twenty-two months she lived on the road, never even checking into a motel. She slept at highway rest stops, woke, sat up, and drove. She knew she'd find them. For fifteen years, she'd lived with that man, and she knew the limits of his imagination. He was a man who considered standard vacation spots obscure. In fifteen years, they'd taken fifteen vacations. To the Grand Canyon, Mt. Rushmore, the Smoky Mountains. How hard could it be? Each day opened like a promise.

She found them in Galveston, looked through the screen door of a cabin he'd rented, and saw her two youngest, then four and six, eating cereal from bowls on the living-room floor. They stood up and pressed their spines against the wall when they saw her, and they wouldn't come near, not even when she whispered their names. Outside, the oldest one,

Frank, who was twelve, must have watched her drive up, because she turned to see him, breathless and possessed, taking a baseball bat to her van. She ran to him, and the younger ones followed, the baby crying, tugging at his brother's clothes as he smashed Joy's headlights, her windshield, her side mirrors.

"What are we doing, Frankie?" the baby screeched. "What are we doing?"

Suddenly Joy's husband was behind them at the screen door shouting, "Franklin Marshall Howard, you stop that."

Frank did, staring wildly at him and then throwing the bat as far as he could. It clattered across the street and wedged in the mouth of a storm drain. Joy took a step toward him, and, though his face was dirty and streaked with tears, she saw the new shadow of a mustache just above his lip. It brought her hand to her own mouth. He ran furiously away from her, cutting behind houses, the two little ones following, pleading after him, "Frankie, Frankie."

Joy's husband stood still in the doorway, but she walked right past him to the van, scooped glass out of her seat, got in, and went after her boys, driving circles through the neighborhood, calling their names through the broken windshield, screaming details of their pasts: "Frankie, you had a blue trike when you were three, with a bell you loved to ring. And Jerry, you ate strawberries every summer from the garden. And in the winter you all three went sledding on Carter's Hill. And Tommy, you were afraid—my baby, my littlest boy—of the mailman and spiders and bees. You *know* me," she called out to them. "I know *you*."

Men stopped in yards as she passed, held rakes. She took a wrong turn and was driving erratically, frantic for a street she recognized, when the police pulled her over. One officer helped her find the house again, but they were already gone, the clothes dryer still running on a back porch off the kitchen.

The story silences the new girl—and us, too. We sit in our

chairs, a curl of smoke rising from Annalise's cigarette. None of us has ever gotten that close: to see our child's face, its features shifted ever so slightly from the arrangement in old snapshots we carry. To watch our child *eat*. To see our child's chest rise and fall in a tremble of breath under a thin T-shirt. For that moment we would forget all the breath that has moved and continues to move them into a future without us. Like Joy, we would call out the details we carry, open our kit bags to remind them of toys and pets and friends and rooms and days they've forgotten. We'd insist they knew us. And, *Sweetie, Scoopalopodus, Ballerinatina*, we'd say, *I know you.* Finally, then, our personal tragedies would fall away. We would be like any parent, every parent, all our children gone, looking for the dead, believing that when we find them they will stare blankly at us, and then, hearing the call of our stories, blink back to life.

VERY SHORT FICTION AWARD
1st-, 2nd-, and 3rd-Place Winners

First-place winner: JANET DESAULNIERS

Janet Desaulniers receives $1200 for her first-place story, "Mothers without Children," which begins on page 31, preceded by her profile on page 30.

Second-place winner: DANIEL VILLASENOR

Daniel Villasenor receives $500 for "Blood." He has an M.F.A. from the University of Arizona, where he received an Academy of American Poets Prize, and he has been a Stegner Fellow in poetry at Stanford. Villasenor lives in Arroyo Seco, New Mexico where he makes his living as a blacksmith, horseshoer, and horsetrainer.

"Blood"

We were all at the table, eating something. My father, my mother, Madeline, and myself. We had been in a comedy of silence for days, as if we had experienced some tragedy together that was too blistered and near the surface to be named. Jacqueline, she said, what is wrong with your husband that he will not even look at me?

Third-place winner: AMY J. MARCOTT

Amy J. Marcott receives $300 for "Villanelle." She received her B.A. from Wesleyan University and will complete her M.F.A. in fiction at the Pennsylvania State University this year. She is currently at work on a novel.

"Villanelle"

Despite her deafness, Meredith is fluent with noise. She rattles the screen on the patio door, stomps her feet, claps her hands. She can make wonderful, chaotic sounds, my daughter. I think of it as sound poetry. Art. If she were a painter I imagine she would be a cubist.

We invite you to our website (www.glimmertrain.com) to see a listing of the top twenty-five winners and finalists. We thank all entrants for sending in their work.

ANDRE DUBUS
Writer

Interview

by Jennifer Levasseur and Kevin Rabalais

Andre Dubus

Andre Dubus is the author of six collections of stories, most recently Dancing After Hours. *A retired Marine Corps captain, Mr. Dubus has also written two novels,* The Lieutenant *and* Voices from the Moon, *and two collections of essays,* Broken Vessels *and* Meditations from a Moveable Chair. *Mr. Dubus has received two Guggenheim fellowships, a MacArthur fellowship, the PEN-Malamud Award, the Rea Award for excellence in short fiction, and the Jean Stein Award from the American Academy of Arts and Letters.*

Jennifer Levasseur and Kevin Rabalais interviewed Mr. Dubus in his home in Haverhill, Massachusetts.

For more than thirty years, you have been publishing short stories almost exclusively. Your first published book, however, The Lieutenant, *was a novel. In the past, you've said that book would have been better as a novella, even though it has all the characteristics of a novel. What would you have changed?*

I looked at *The Lieutenant* in the eighties because a small press reprinted it, and I had to read the galleys. I wouldn't have cut it then because they wanted to print it as it was, and because I couldn't figure how to change it. I don't remember that novel, but I suspect I could have compressed some of it. I could not at twenty-nine have compressed more, though. If I had written it twelve years later, maybe I could have. Maybe I would have had fewer scenes. I couldn't have made it twenty pages, but maybe one hundred and twenty. I was learning while writing that novel.

You began a second novel, which was later abandoned, after the publication of The Lieutenant. *Did any stories grow from that novel?*

I had actually written a novel before *The Lieutenant.* I finally burned it after eighteen drafts because I had outgrown it. After *The Lieutenant* was published, I started one, and I think I was on the second chapter when I read a story by Chekhov called "Peasants." It covers one family, one village, and one year in thirty pages. I went for a drive in New Hampshire, and when I came back, I read it again and thought, I have to learn how to compress. I never looked back again. No, I didn't get any stories out of that novel.

Shortly after the publication of The Lieutenant, *you wrote a screenplay based on the novel.*

I wrote two drafts of a bad screenplay a year later and was paid.

What kind of exercise was that for you?

It was so easy, and I think that is why it was such a bad screenplay. The producer said, "Go home and write the kind of movie you would like to see." After I finished, he said, "There is too much dialogue. You're thinking like a novelist. Ninety percent of this would be cut because the actors would express this with their bodies."

Would you have liked to see it made into a film?

I still would. I think it would make a good movie, and I could use the money.

Several of your characters reappear throughout the stories. What do you feel are the advantages of having recurring characters in stories, rather than using these characters in a longer work?

I do sometimes plan to have several stories with the same character, but I have never thought of the advantages. It could be a limitation; I don't know. I prefer reading stories. Francois Mauriac said, "I don't know why anybody writes long novels. You could always write another novel about the same people."

How do you know when a character will stay with you for more than one story?

Well, I wrote a series about a boy, Paul Clement, in Louisiana, and I knew I would write about him. When I got older and looked back at those stories, I realized those weren't my parents; those were my memories of how I saw them when I was ten. The stories always changed anyway. There were also those three novellas—"We Don't Live Here Anymore," "Adultery," and "Finding a Girl in America"—and I did not think there would be three. I wrote "We Don't Live Here Anymore," and I started worrying about the character Edith. I think she's the only one in those stories I liked. Then I wrote "Adultery." I was writing "Finding a Girl in America," a story about a man whose girlfriend aborts his child, and I decided to put Hank Allison in there. There were also some Peter Jackman stories. I don't think I knew he would get three stories. There are several LuAnn Arceneaux stories in *Dancing After Hours*. Those were a mess to get going. I used her when I decided to write a story about how two people meet, because that always fascinates me. I knew I would try "Out of the Snow" with LuAnn. The idea for that one came from an experience I had when I was picking up my youngest daughters one day. I was in my wheelchair, and I saw a big boy pushing a smaller boy around. I started to drive away, but then I thought, I can't just let this happen. I drove back and said, "You stop that, or I'll call the police." What else could I do? Another guy came up and said, "It's okay, mister. Don't call the police. That guy said something about his sister." I said, "That guy's too big. He shouldn't be doing that." I then thought about how I shouldn't disturb the police over something so foolish. But a woman came up behind me and spoke before dispersing them. And then I thought, why not write a story about a woman dealing with violence?

Do you still read novels, or do you concentrate more on stories?

I still read novels. I recently pulled out Mauriac and Balzac's *Cousin Bette*, but I got interrupted by baseball season. I like to reread novels. I'm in the mood to read some more of Graham Greene's novels. I'm not sure I like stories more than novels; it just depends on who the writer is.

Do you ever think about writing novels again?

Oh, God forbid. No, no.

Your stories are driven by character, and you've said your characters often control the fate of the story.

In my story "Miranda over the Valley," the character gets so bitter, and I kept rewriting the ending, but she kept doing the same thing.

It sounds like you feel your characters hold the ultimate responsibility.

Yes. I only got nineteen words today, and I don't even know what the characters are doing in this story I'm writing. I've got to take a couple days off until they show me something. If I would have finished that section today, I would have been screwed. It's a new section, and I don't know what's going on, so I'll take a few days off and then see what happens.

So do you see your characters as somewhere outside your mind? Where do they come from?

I think they come from their actions and what they are thinking and feeling. My job is to figure out what they are feeling. I will have a physical description and some history in my head before I start a story. I'm writing a western now, and I know this character who is a black cowboy in Southern California. I know his family went from Chicago to California during the gold rush, and his father set up a church in Los Angeles. That's not the story, but I know that.

Do you feel you know more about your characters, even things that don't get put into the stories?

I want to know about their religion, their sensual habits, how they feel about death, life, where they are from, whom they are kin to. But that's not always what I get to know. I'm thinking about my story "Dancing After Hours." All I had with the female character was her age and that she thought she was not pretty. I don't know where she's from, and I don't know anything about her family. Since she doesn't mention much about religion, I assume that is not part of her life.

If I can finish this western, I'm going to try this one again: a Catholic family, French one side, Irish, the other, with a martyred nun. I wanted to have her martyred in El Salvador. I either copped out, or I made a tactical decision. I've never been to El Salvador, and I don't know any Spanish. I thought, why go through all that work to find a violent country when we live in such a violent country? I try to see the characters, to know some of their history. I will think about characters for a long time rather than just start the story and see what they do. I like to feel I can get inside of a character. I used to tell students to write sketches. I told them they should know if their character prefers a bath or a shower. I like to think I know that. Now, with this story I'm writing set in 1891, they don't take many baths. This is a sequel to one I wrote last year, and nobody has taken a bath yet.

One thing you do when writing a story is to read drafts into a recorder. When did you begin this exercise?

I was at Iowa, and I don't know who told me about this wonderful idea. And then, one of my kids dropped the tape recorder, and I couldn't replace it. Several years later I got another one, and I've been doing it ever since. It's a great thing to do.

What do you feel this allows during your editing process?

I think I see things I didn't see before. Sometimes I've read paragraphs a hundred times, but I think reading aloud allows me to get physical and use my body so I can see mistakes more clearly. I cut a lot this way. It helps to check dialogue: Is this the wrong rhythm? Are these repetitions? I hear things that I don't see when I do this. I read it in a very dull way. When I listen to it, it's even less interesting. It's not passionate. I don't read it dramatically. I just read it. If you heard the tapes, you would say, "This man's working." It's not like I'm reading my work in front of an audience.

How, other than reading into the recorder, do you edit your work?

I write slowly, and I try to edit as much as I can while I'm writing. The next day, I'll read from the beginning, so I'm doing it all over again. I don't read it when I'm finished that day. I put it aside and don't think about it until the next day.

Your novella "Adultery" went through seven drafts before it was published. There were a total of four hundred pages from the drafts, and the final version appears at sixty pages. How did you compress this novella?

The first draft was a short novel, and it was terrible. It was embarrassing. Nobody ever saw that one. It never got out of longhand. The idea came from two articles in the newspaper. I think I read them in the same summer. One was about a guy who was traveling on the highway with his wife at night in

Massachusetts. He stopped to get gasoline, and while the tank was getting filled, he went into the bathroom. His wife woke up, and she decided to go to the bathroom, too. He came out, and he didn't know she had gone, so he drove away without her. The state troopers got him and brought him back. The other story was about a young guy who got an internship with the *Boston Globe*, and he was hitchhiking from Washington State to Boston. A trucker who was dying of cancer picked him up. The trucker was driving around drinking beer and smoking cigarettes and talking into a microphone to his family, but he didn't have it connected because he didn't want them to watch him die. So then I thought, let's put Hank and Edith in this story. I had them go to Mexico. He drives off the road to go to the bathroom, and she crosses the highway and hitchhikes back with a trucker who dies in Maine. There was a funeral scene, and the whole thing was just awful. And then I got to work, and he disappeared.

It was a long process. I thought I had a draft finished in the early stages, and then I realized it wasn't done. One time it was much shorter, and it almost worked on several occasions.

Voices from the Moon was also an idea that came from a newspaper story. Does this happen often?

That story came from the *Boston Globe*, too. Maybe I should be reading the paper more now. I guess several stories have come from the paper. There is a story in *Dancing After Hours* called "Blessings," and I got that idea from the paper.

Do you do all your own research?

Yes, I do. For this western, for instance, the next thing I have to do is call a music store and find out what would be a nice waltz to play on the gramophone in 1891. There's not a lot of necessary research in my work, but if I have to I do it. There's always somebody to ask, and people like to tell you about their work.

After over thirty years of publishing, how have your ideas of what fiction should accomplish changed?

I want to use physical details and spiritual light and darkness in such a way that a reader experiences them and becomes the character, goes through what the character goes through. But when I'm writing, I always become the character. I just go through the story with the character to see what is going to happen.

You served in the Marine Corps, and in 1964 you left as a captain. Were there similarities between the community of men on the ship you were stationed on and the community of writers when you moved to join the Iowa Writers Workshop?

There was some immediate shock. It was very different. In the Marine Corps, I didn't talk about writing. Teaching was a lateral move. There were similarities between that and the Marine Corps. To be in a room full of writers and not hide that you were writing was a very exciting thing for me, and I hadn't experienced that until Iowa.

Had you hid that you were writing during your period in the Marines?

Well, I didn't go around telling everybody. I had my first story published when I was in the Marine Corps, and there was nobody to tell. I couldn't just go knock on the major's door and say, "I wanted to tell you …"

Would that have been looked down upon at that time?

No. Actually, that was some kind of narcissism in my head from school days. My son Andre III, who is a writer, and I were talking about this. We were the ones who thought the guys thought this wasn't a guy thing to do. The guys didn't think that. I told him, "Good athletes used to ask me to help them with their school work. All I had to do was ask them to help me throw a football, and they would have been happy to." And he agreed. There was a gunnery sergeant I was very close to, and he found out I sold the story and said, "I want to read it." It was just my own self-absorption. Of course it wouldn't have been a problem.

Were you thinking at that time that writing could be a career?

I never thought it would be a money-making career. I thought I would have to stay in the Marine Corps for twenty years at that time. I thought I didn't want to teach, but then I resigned from the Marine Corps, and I began teaching, which I always enjoyed very much.

You taught modern fiction at Bradford College for eighteen years. What writers did you teach?

There were many I enjoyed teaching. I did seminars, but they would change from time to time. Once it was Hemingway, and another time it was South African writers, but I couldn't find many in those days. Nadine Gordimer and Andre Brink I could find without a problem. I couldn't find many blacks, and the blacks I was able to find were not very good. I guess it was because they hadn't been able to read much. I can't remember his name, but there was one black writer I taught whose stories were not good because of the rage, but the rage was good. I had a Southern literature course I really enjoyed. I started with Faulkner's *Go Down, Moses*, and we spent six weeks on it. I wouldn't leave a page of "The Bear" until we all understood it. I went from pre-Civil War to *The Moviegoer*. I went from *Go Down, Moses* to Chopin's *The Awakening*, and then there was *Lie Down in Darkness*, and so on. The course went through time and place. I taught Chekhov, Joyce's *Dubliners*, Isaac Babel, Kafka's stories, Raymond Carver's stories. I stopped using anthologies at one point, and sometimes I would teach stories and novels I hadn't read. I certainly did teach Graham Greene.

Aside from the literature courses, you also taught creative writing. Did you enjoy teaching one more than the other?

They're very different, and I think I enjoyed teaching them equally. Literature was scarier to teach because I had to hope something would happen in the course. In fiction workshops,

I just had to respond to what somebody else did.

What would you say you've learned about reading and writing through teaching?

I could never list the things because the students were good. I learned to stop defining stories and telling people what they are about, because to each student, the story is what happens to her on that page. If she's got a good reason, then she's right. The students' writing was always stimulating. Every day I was hearing sentences that had never been written.

Many of your stories are written in third person. Is this a conscious choice you've made in your body of work?

It is a conscious choice. When I write in first person, I tend to be too wordy. The narrators just take off. I think I need third-person narration. First-person narrators, when I'm writing them, tend to tell everything. I don't even know the last time I've tried using first-person narrators in stories, but I've written many first-person essays.

Do you approach the writing of essays differently than the writing of fiction?

They are very different. The first difference is point of view. I've really got to squeeze it to make sure it doesn't wander all over the place. It's not the same kind of excitement with an essay. I always know what is going to happen because they've all happened to me, whereas with the stories, I don't know what is going to happen; there is an element of suspense. Other than that, when I'm writing the sentences it feels about the same. No, that's not true. If you write about a black cowboy beating up a white racist, it's a whole lot different from writing a sentence about something that happened to you and your children, as far as the rush is concerned.

It seems you use material from your life, judging by some similarities between personal essays and stories. I'm thinking of the essay from Meditations from a Moveable Chair *titled "Giving Up the Gun" and a story from* Dancing After Hours *called "The Intruder."*

That's interesting. I wrote "The Intruder" aboard ship in 1961, and that's the story the *Sewanee Review* took while I was in the Marine Corps. Richard Yates read the story, and he liked it. Through the years, when my collections were being published, he would always say, "Why don't you put 'The Intruder' in there?" A year after he died, I started thinking about "The Intruder" again. I said, "Dick is talking to me." I was working on *Dancing After Hours*, so I took "The Intruder" out and read it, and it was like looking at a picture of myself when I was seven. So I sent it to my editor, and I said, "This may look like I'm trying to fill up the book, but the truth is I think Yates is talking to me." Sure, I take raw material from my life, but that story was all made up.

Dialect is rarely dealt with in your stories.

I don't use it, and I don't care much to read it. I have no dialect in this western I'm working on now. I decided before I started that the black man was going to speak normally; he would not have any kind of accent that would denote slavery or anything else; he's educated, and everybody in the story would just speak normally as they do in Chekhov. I like dialect in the right hands. Faulkner did beautiful things with language. Sometimes he wrote a line that sounded more like dialogue than read like it. There was a voice he developed that made this so, I think. No good writer's dialogue ever sounds good in a tape recorder.

What was your process in selecting stories for The Selected Stories of Andre Dubus?

The editor selected most of them. He came out to the house one day, and while we were going through the stories, he said, "I'm going to put *Voices from the Moon* in there. Nobody read that story, and I'm going to put it right in the middle." He did the arranging. I don't have a clue about arranging stories. With the newest collection, all I knew was that I wanted "Dancing After Hours" last.

Were you happy with the way The Selected Stories *turned out?*
Yes. I think he did a good job. I was looking through there
the other day to see if anything is missing. I should talk to
someone at Knopf about collecting some of the novellas and
longer stories.

Speaking of Voices from the Moon, *it was marketed as a novel
upon publication, rather than a novella or long story.*
That was a very funny period. We had a gentleman's argument, and I could have said no to calling it a novel. But we had
a debate, and you can't win that kind of debate. I kept saying,
"*Play It as It Lays* by Joan Didion is a novel. It takes about as
long to read as *Voices from the Moon*, but my book is a novella."
If we were in France, it wouldn't even be a debate. A woman
in my workshop said, "I don't know why you don't call
yourself a novelist. You would be in Japan or France." *Voices
from the Moon* came really nicely to me, not easily. It's never
easy—but it just came out. I'm not sure it took longer than a
summer.

Your novel The Lieutenant *took about the same amount of time
to write. Now you say your stories take longer. What is the difference
in pacing between your writing then and now?*
I'm not sure if I knew how to bear down then. I'm not sure
if full concentration came to me during the writing of *The
Lieutenant*. I was writing what I call horizontally, making
scenes go. In my forties, I switched to vertically, trying to get
inside a world and inside a character. Of course, the book was
based on a story that actually happened. I changed the events
a little to make the novel. I told the story so many times, and
somebody said I should write it. That started in first person,
too. I gave a chapter to my wife, and then realized I was
writing everything that happened as I remembered it, every
detail from the ship. I started over in third person. First person
feels like talking to me.

Your essays are all written in the first person, and they are very short.

I really bear down with the essays. I saw a nice review in the *Philadelphia Enquirer*. The reviewer said, "Hemingway is an influence more than ever before in these personal essays." I said, "He may be right." They are very hard to write, and it's hard to keep from launching into a monologue about my life.

You've been critical of some fiction editors of magazines. You've also said, half-jokingly, you feel the two worst things for a young writer are literature professors and the New Yorker. *What do you think is the role of an editor of a magazine?*

I think their role is to say yes or no and not try to change the story. Finding mistakes, maybe suggesting to cut a line, that's all right. I've gotten weird letters from editors. One place wanted "The Timing of Sin," but the editors wanted the whole story to take place somewhere else, cutting the story in half. They thought they wanted the story, but they didn't. They wanted the story they thought they saw. I think it's a bad thing to tempt a young writer because young writers want recognition, and the magazine is waving the check, which won't do anybody any good anyway in the long run. I had a friend who was studying at the University of Arkansas in Fayetteville, and he called and said a buddy of his had just sold his first story to the *New Yorker*. He said they made him change it from a Southern voice in first person to a neutral voice. I said, "Why did he change it?" He said, "Thirty-five hundred dollars." I said, "He's a graduate student. He can't go to Mexico for a year. He can't even buy a car. You know why he did that? Because nobody cares what anybody writes. You'd like to be able to walk into a bar in Akron, Ohio, and have the guy next to you say, 'What do you do?' and you say, 'I write.' He says, 'You been published?' and you say, 'Yeah, the *New Yorker.*'" It's not the money that's a bad influence; it's their need to rewrite the story. And regarding literature professors, some of them go nuts on reading into things and, in turn, they ruin the purity and spontaneity of readers. They make literature some removed thing.

How do you feel about taking advice from colleagues or members of your writers workshop?

I like it if I respect the person. If the person is right, then yes. Gary Fisketjon at Knopf had some suggestions for *Dancing After Hours*. I had a story called "Andromache" that was in the *New Yorker*, and that was a good letter, a good editor. He sent the rejection, and I showed it to a wonderful writer named Thomas Williams who said, "I haven't read the story, but this is a very interesting letter; maybe you should read it again." He was right. I had been reading too much William Styron. There were flashbacks inside flashbacks and vortexes and this and that, and I didn't need that. I wrote that story again, and it was better. I said to Tom Williams, "I wrote part of that story for myself. Some of it has nothing to do with anything, but what do I do?" He said, "Well, you just put it in the drawer and cry until you can use it somewhere else."

How do you feel about the market for stories right now?

I think it's great. There are all these quarterlies. I keep telling writers, "If you keep it in the mail, somebody will take it." I was talking to a French literary agent in the eighties, and he said, "We don't have literary magazines for stories and poetry. There are only two, and they commission pieces." I don't know about other countries, but you just have to persist. I don't believe a good story will go unpublished.

Many publishers seem to be leery of trying to publish books of stories.

It's hard to publish any kind of book these days. I have a friend who has worked in bookstores for years, and he says new books of stories come out all the time. I just endorsed one this year by Mark Slouka called *Lost Lake*, and it's wonderful. It's always been true that publishers would rather have a novel than a collection of stories. Americans, for some reason, don't seem to be reading books of stories, but is that really true? I think today Hemingway and Fitzgerald would publish books of stories between novels. I believe their stories would have been published anyway, as well as Faulkner's. But publishers have always preferred novels.

In a review of The Times Are Never So Bad, *Joyce Carol Oates said, "The stories read more like excerpts from longer works than stories complete in themselves." What is your definition of a story?*

I stopped having them. I had a student named Michael Bussey, and my system for undergraduates was that every other week, they had to come in with five longhand pages and read them. I told the students they could go both semesters without completing a story, as long as they were working. I feel anybody who assigns three stories in a semester doesn't respect the form, because a story may take three years to write and you can't hurry it. I told them to keep working. As it turned out, around March the finished stories started coming in, and every other week, Michael read a complete story. In the fall semester, I started thinking of them as sketches. By the end of the year, I saw he had written nine beautiful stories, stories about a little boy and his brother, and he followed the boy until age nineteen. I said, "Michael, I'm never going to call a story a sketch again. I used to think these were sketches, but now I think a story is what feels like a story." So that's what I think, and I'm not sure what Joyce Carol Oates meant. Maybe they were excerpts from longer works and the rest of them didn't come to me; I don't know.

Themes run throughout your work, where the same idea repeats itself. Do you revisit scenes or sections of dialogue because you feel you've reached a new understanding of the matter?

It's not intentional. I knew I had written about abortion, for instance, in "Finding a Girl in America," and I didn't look at it again. I didn't want to go back in that direction in "Falling in Love" in *Dancing After Hours*. I told a priest who is in the workshop about my situation, and I said, "I've got another abortion story, and I've already gone there twice in stories. Do I have to go back again?" He said, "Yes." So I did. That doesn't bother me. There's a lot of repetition in a lot of writers I love, probably because of their passions, fears, what we love as humans. It doesn't bother me; it's just unintentional.

You've said you don't outline stories. Do you outline your essays?

No. I'll do something similar to an outline, though, in the notebook I'm writing in. Take *Voices from the Moon*, for instance. Before I started it, I worked it out so it started one morning and ended later that night. I knew the sections would have alternating points of view, and I knew the young boy would control the point of view for every other section, because it's his story. I chose which sections would have which character's point of view. I wouldn't call that an outline, but I guess you could. I just said, "This is where people will be." I make notes in the margin when something comes to me.

In your essay "Selling Stories" from Broken Vessels, *you say you became used to rejections from magazines at a young age, that you learned to accept them. However, you say it's different with a book publisher.*

The rejections that really hurt during that period after I wrote *The Lieutenant* were not the rejection slips that said, "I don't like the collection of stories," but the ones that said, "We'll publish this collection of stories if you write a novel." That hurt. I thought I was being told to be somebody else. I became immune to rejections by the time I got out of college, long before I had anything published. I started to send out stories when I was eighteen because I knew I had to develop a thick skin.

In that same essay you also say, "There is no one to sell out to as a story writer." Has this been one of the reasons you've continued to write stories?

I just don't see novels. I still think *The Lieutenant* is an idea for a short novella. I've written shorter things about more complicated things, but I don't get ideas for novels, and that's why I don't write them. I don't know how anybody does. My son Andre does, and he goes off for five years into this world and then comes up with a new world he's made.

How do you feel about your son's decision to become a writer?

I love it.

Much of your work is dedicated to your children. How do they respond to your writing?

They tell me they like it. The young girls haven't read it yet. I think it's just something Dad does. My oldest daughter, when I published *The Lieutenant*, was nine years old. She was very happy and curious that her dad didn't go to work every morning, but that he went to classes three days a week and then came home and wrote, and I felt the same way.

You recently switched to publishing with Knopf after many years with Godine.

I was in my last year of a MacArthur Foundation grant, and I wasn't going to be able to afford the mortgage. The accountant said, "This is real. You will lose the house." I was feeling very low, and then I realized I had to stop waiting for guys with suits to do something, that I needed to call my agent. I called and said, "I've got to go free agent. I can't be loyal to anybody. I'm going to lose my damn house." My agent said, "This will be fun." So I got a two-year contract, and my house is paid for. I'm glad I did it. I'm very happy with Knopf. As long as I had income, I didn't need to do it, but things change.

Every Thursday night since the fall of 1987, a writers workshop has met at your house. How did this come about?

In the fall of '87, a woman from south of Boston called. She said she had eight writers who wanted to pay a couple hundred dollars each for four nights of a workshop. And then ten writers gave a benefit for me that winter. I thought, Well, all those writers gave me that, so I'm not going to charge writers until I have to. I said, "Come up and I'll see what you are doing." So they came over, and I talked to each one, and I said, "It looks like we need a workshop." So that's how it began. There's been a major rotation over ten years. We have a twenty-seven-year-old who hasn't been here much because she's in Harvard at the business school. One woman has published a novel; another is publishing stories in quarterlies. There's another woman in her seventies who is publishing. They're pretty much in their thirties and forties, most of them, with jobs and families.

Bradford was a women's college when you taught there. You've said in the past that women are better writers than men. Do you still feel this way?

Did I say that? I do read a lot of women writers. We came to Massachusetts for the geography. We had never been here. Women are the ones who read books. But I don't think women are better writers than men. They're different. I said in a class at Bradford, "Updike writes like a woman," and the women got upset. I said, "It's not an insult. A man goes into a room in a strange house he's never been to, and when he comes out he doesn't know what he saw. His wife will go in, and she will know the wallpaper, the curtains, the furniture, and every detail of the house. But the guy will come out and say, 'Well, they were nice people.'" I didn't know what was in my house until I got confined to it. I couldn't tell you what color the walls were. Women are very sensuous. I have a group of abused teenagers I meet with every Monday night, and one of them asked to read some women writers. She said, "Let's read some Virginia Woolf." I said, "All the women writers I read are too complicated and lyrical and too sexy. I'm just not going to read them in here." In that group, we mostly read Tobias Wolff and Hemingway, stuff like that with sentences that are approachable. When a woman writer gets on a roll, boy, you get lost.

What have you been reading lately?

At line yesterday while I was getting my driver's license renewed, I started reading Dennis Lehane's new novel, *Gone, Baby, Gone*. I was reading *Cousin Bette* and loving it, but something interrupted me. I hope it was something like swimming or baseball. I finally gave it up and put it back on the shelf. I read a novel in manuscript by my middle sister last week. So the truth is that if I can keep up with family and friends, that's about all I can do.

Are any of your other family members writing?

My oldest daughter is working on a screenplay. She can write well. My fourth child, who is a therapist in Santa Cruz, has written two novels, but neither one has been published. They can all write. My sixteen-year-old came over with my eleven-year-old, and we were all in the pool. I looked up and the older one was gone. I said, "Where's Cadence?" My daughter Madeline said, "She's writing a story." I said, "That's a serious sixteen-year-old."

I got a little burned out reading. When I was teaching at the University of Alabama, I bought Marguerite Duras's *The Lover*. When I began reading it, all of a sudden it felt like it weighed two hundred pounds, and I had to put it down. I was going to reread *War and Peace* for the third time last fall. Then I thought, "It will be the World Series. You are going to read twelve pages a day." So I bought a six-volume video with Anthony Hopkins made for BBC, and it's the most magnificent thing I've ever seen in my life. I decided watching the film version wasn't a cop-out because I've taught the book and love it and always will. I'm lonely at night, and something about picking up a book at night makes me lonely, but videos don't. I don't know why that's true.

Are there any stories you are most proud of?

They are mostly gone when I finish them. I remember the

ones that were hardest to write. "Adultery" was hard, and I almost quit writing it a few times. "Dancing After Hours" was very hard, as well. I am fond of many of the stories in *The Last Worthless Evening*. I like "Molly" and "Deaths at Sea."

"Deaths at Sea" is one of the few stories that deals with racism. Did you make a decision to stay away from the topic?

There should be more. This western I wrote last summer deals with it, and the sequel I'm working on now deals with it because the main character is black. But I don't know the answer. In the sixties and seventies, I shied away from writing about this topic because of the turmoil in our country. It probably just hasn't come up in the stories. I guess I haven't been writing about characters who are racist.

You just mentioned your story "Molly," which is a powerful story of a girl moving into adulthood and confronting her own sexuality. How did that story come to you?

That story was hard. It started from the point of view of a fishing captain who first sees the mother, Claire. It started on his fishing boat off the New Hampshire coast. Claire invites him over to her house for dinner. He's the first one who sees Molly. I didn't know how to finish it, and then a couple days later I realized it was finished, and that I just needed an epilogue. I wrote that epilogue with my daughter Cadence, who was three years old at the time, on my lap.

In your essay "After Twenty Years," you say you've "always known that writing fiction had little effect on the world; that if it did, young men would not have gone to war after the Iliad." What do you feel a writer's role is in society?

I hate to tell you. Somebody wrote me about that essay, and she said, "It helps those of us who do read to help those who don't." And I think that's what reading does, but it doesn't get things done. Caesar Chavez did more than six John Steinbecks could have done. Workers don't own their own lives yet. It must have helped in communist countries, but it doesn't help in capitalistic societies. Have you ever seen any good come because somebody wrote a book of fiction? Individual good, yes. I think it's a limited effort, a beautiful effort that is a gift from God. I think people should do it and make music and paintings. I just wish the world would get better for everybody and there would be true democracy. Literature touches individual lives. It comforts, soothes, and delights. It turns us on, enrages us. I think the average life span in Haiti is forty or forty-five. Graham Greene wrote *The Comedians* about Haiti, and that's a wonderful book. When the day comes that a politician picks up a novel and sees the light, I'm just going to walk straight to heaven. I think art is for the individual soul. I never read Thomas More's *Utopia*. A woman I know read it, and she said, "There are no artists in there." I was educated by Christian brothers, and a wise Jesuit once told me, "If there were no sins, there wouldn't be art." At the least, stories are fun to read. 🏃

Jennifer Levasseur and Kevin Rabalais are working on a series of interviews with American writers. They live in New Orleans.

Andre Dubus died February 24, 1999, in Haverhill,
Massachusetts, at the age of sixty-three.

Siobhan Dowd of International PEN's Writers-in-Prison Committee in London writes this column regularly, alerting readers to the plight of writers around the world who deserve our awareness and our writing action.

Writer Detained: Xu Wenli
by Siobhan Dowd

*T*he Chinese President, Jiang Zemin, when recently celebrating the twentieth anniversary of a set of economic reforms, stated that the political system "must not be rocked," and attempts to do so would be "nipped in the bud." As if to underscore this point, several dissidents, all of whom were try-

Xu Wenli

ing to propose a more flexible approach to the country's politics, were arrested. One of these was the veteran editor, writer, and human-rights activist Xu Wenli. His subsequent

Glimmer Train Stories, Issue 31, Summer 1999
© 1999 Siobhan Dowd

sentencing to thirteen years dismayed but did not surprise the international human-rights community. "A human-rights treaty signed by China isn't worth the paper it's written on," was the dry comment of Sidney Jones of Human Rights Watch.

Xu, aged fifty-five, is originally from Anqing in Anhui Province. He describes in an autobiographical account of his childhood how desperately he had wanted to be a writer, but after his father, a Red Army doctor, met with a sudden and fatal accident, his schooling abruptly ceased. On reaching adulthood, he joined the air force, then moved to Beijing, where he worked as an electrician and settled down with his wife and daughter.

This peaceful existence was shattered when the Beijing Spring movement of the late 1970s gathered pace; Xu decided that he wished to add his weight to the momentum for change. He set up and edited an unofficial but influential journal, *April Fifth Tribune,* named for a demonstration against Mao's Cultural Revolution on April 5, 1976. It appeared for about eighteen months before pressure from the authorities forced it to close. As the authorities clamped down on dissent, Xu was arrested in 1981 and sentenced to fifteen years' imprisonment. The indictment accused him of failing to edit out reference to the "bloody" dictatorship of the proletariat, but Xu and others believed that his conviction really arose from his defense of Wei Jingsheng, another prominent dissident who had lately been jailed. Whatever the case, the following example of Xu's editorial style shows clearly how very outspoken he was, even for that brief time of candor:

> Some people say that the main thing now is to work to modernize China and that there will be time to discuss civil rights after that. For the time being we shouldn't bother about affairs of state. But in that case how are the people to express

their power? Is the aim to turn the Chinese into conveyor-belt workers, like in Chaplin's *Modern Times*? What then is the point of human intelligence? Ever since there has been a more open policy towards the outside world, Chinese intellectuals have been unable to go abroad. Many have not come back. That is a very clear sign. A person who cannot think freely feels wounded. Only a minority are allowed to express their views. It is impossible to modernize the country unless you let the intelligence of a thousand million individuals unfold.

In 1985, four years into his prison term, an extraordinary, handwritten document entitled "My Self-Defence" reached the West.

It was identified as being by Xu and had been smuggled out, apparently with the connivance of one of the prison administrators. In it, Xu portrayed his trial as a farce, and described how he had stunned the courtroom by suggesting that the judge should recuse himself. Not long after the manuscript was published in the West, Xu was transferred to a solitary, windowless cell, the sole access to which was through a trapdoor, and was deprived of family visits.

In 1993, three years ahead of time, he was released. "I committed no crime," he said as he emerged from his prison cell. "What I did, I did for my country. There is a pop song called 'I'm Still the Same Old Me.' I think that best describes my meaning." Sure enough, Xu, after a brief break, resumed his dissident activities. He met with members of the foreign press and attempted to found a new party, the Chinese Democratic Party. His attempts to have the party formally registered were unsuccessful, however. He attracted significant media attention in the UK when he was arrested during Tony Blair's visit to China last year. Blair intervened on his behalf and, perhaps as a result, he was quickly released.

However, he was not to remain free for long. On December 1, 1998, he was detained as a "criminal suspect"; his house was raided, his documents, address books, videos, and fax machine were confiscated; within three weeks he had been tried and convicted for subversion. Specifically, he was accused of "secretly planning" to set up branches of the Chinese Democratic Party and of accepting money for these purposes from abroad. He was given less than four days to prepare a defense and reportedly remained defiantly silent throughout the proceedings until the verdict was handed down, after which he simply observed, "This is political persecution." An official Chinese news agency commented that his heavy thirteen-year sentence had been inflicted because Xu was a repeat offender.

Readers are urged to add their weight to international efforts on Xu Wenli's behalf by writing letters calling for his release to:

> His Excellency Jiang Zemin
> President
> State Council
> Beijing 100032
> People's Republic of China
> Fax: 011 86 10 6512 5810

Robert Chibka

Last-minute Father's Day shopping, 1957. I'd chosen a less showy shirt. The news photographer trawling the men's department for human interest (he perked up at our surname: Dad was famous for his entertaining weekday-morning radio forecasts direct from the Weather Bureau) said this pricier plaid would reproduce better in pointillist halftone photogravure. Mom sprang for the difference. I don't recall whether we gave Dad his gifts before or after he read the paper.

Robert Chibka teaches creative writing and eighteenth-century novels at Boston College. He has written numerous critical articles on Fielding, Sterne, Aphra Behn, Borges, Hawthorne, and Edward Young for various scholarly journals. His first novel, *A Slight Lapse*, was published by W.W. Norton in 1990, and he is at work on a second, *Rigid Liquids*.

Chibka grew up in Portland, Maine, "in the nicest family in the hemisphere (western, northern, take your pick)," and went to school at Yale, Iowa, and Cornell. He currently lives in Boston with his life partner, Marj DeVault, who lives and teaches in Syracuse.

ROBERT CHIBKA
Thrift

Getting and spending, we lay waste our powers
—Wordsworth,
"The World Is Too Much with Us"

*S*o I was eyeballing the wants. It's amazing what you can run across and, with luck, end up owning. Plenty of items you won't want, too—bass amps, used mower blades, like-new fitness equipment—well, nobody can take an interest in everything. But you can crave something, not knowing what, and then see the ad—I don't know, a power sander—next thing you know, it's yours. Even if you don't have uses in mind, it could be a comfort to have one, in case, you never know, some power-sanding requirement should arise, and you'd be stuck with retail, or renting. My opinion: that's the worst, paying for time instead of the thing itself.

Some publications overclassify so you won't run into an article unless you already know you want it. Isn't that why yellow pages were invented? I mean, why would you look under "Power Tools—Retail" without an immediate requisite for items of this ilk? People don't walk around thinking, Sander, sander, that's the ticket, unless they carpent for a living. Maybe at a sale—yard, garage, tag, rummage, lawn—you see a sizable jar for 99¢, of, say, garlic powder. Before you know it, you're set on the garlic-powder front for an extended period: years. It's not the powder, but the jar's size, or just the 99 itself, that perks you up. (This actually happened, so I know.) You wouldn't pore over Linnaean classifications of, like, "Seasonings—Pulverized." But with this item merged into sundry others' midst, you have such an opportunity.

Granted, you draw a line at personals. You don't need to get distracted by SWFs or GBMs when you're on the trail of one standard consumer good or another. In most mainstream periodicals, everybody's pretty similar anyway, interested in nature, dinner, music of some kind, and senses of humor, increasingly not going for smokers, drinkers, and what they define as weirdos, feeling positive about sincerity, sometimes animals, less commonly children. (You figure those who single out kids have some but prefer not to say so in the first-impression market; they get it on the record without coming right out.) Omit liking youngsters or pets and reviling tobacco slash alcohol, and it's like horoscope umbrellas: one size fits all. Might as well say, I enjoy enjoying. I mean, you're expected to pick a life-mate on the grounds that they like candles with their food?

So personals have to be their own category; likewise building materials in quantity, and offspring supplies, a waste of time for the rest of us. Beyond that, the value of overly subdividing goods fails to occur to me off the crack of the bat. I picked up an 8-track deck when it was the last thing on planet Earth I'd have listed as a desire. Now I'm on the constant lookout for tapes. (These are one good deal, too, though you wade through a lot of Pat Boone Xmases and Kiss—often with wrinkly labels making the faces even creepier; what do people listen in, the tub?—to locate tunes that might interest you.) This kind of surprise, it's like a gift, the true pleasure of the wants: discovering urges and fulfilling them in the same swoop. I'd call it the "Seasoning—Pulverized" of life.

So I'm browsing along—truckload of filefolders with discontinued proportions; electric fan, needs work, but comes with a spare propeller—when I notice I'm riveted to this comforter ad. Really, how you say it matters as much as anything. *Quilt* or *coverlet*, I don't guess I'd have given the time of day. But *comforter* sounded so, I don't know ... appealing. And I hate how they get so detailed: "72 x 48, 65/35 poly/cot, lrge flrl (peony?), wdng gft, unconsumtd, per annul agrmnt: she got bed, I linens."

This one just said: "Comforter f/sale, mostly blue, 773-5654 keep trying." I liked that: an encouraging word to strangers from a person who's out a good deal.

I got this phone off a gold-necklaced guy still mourning disco, also trying to unload a ten-speed (trick knee? hemorrhoids? it wasn't my place to ask). It's hotdog shaped, numbers in the bun where the dog sits when idle. A joke from his ex, he said; he already has one with clock radio plus snooze, so he'll let the hotdog go at bottom dollar. One of its features (besides muting, which, living solo, I don't need) is, press #0 and it tries again. This keep-trying ad looked custom-made for my hotdog memory. The phone has a zigzag of nonslip plastic mustard, because otherwise it's round (also nicely curved, ear to mouth, like it's already grilled; well of course, if the mustard's on). Fingering this stripe, though a tad canary for my taste, I'm mighty self-pleased, which makes my prior point: who'd have thought I need wienie-shaped telecommunications?

The numbers are yellowish green pickle-relish bits. I poke them in sequence with the Frank-o-Phone up to my ear because I enjoy the tones: *poo poo pee pah pee pah poo.* It's ringing, and of course no one's there because this is my initial effort, a token gesture to establish intent. I hang up with anticipatudinal relish at using my feature later.

There was no "machine," as people call it now, and I liked

that. Sometimes I think I'm the only holdout against this tidal wave of tape recording. I wondered if they had a principled revulsion like myself or were just elderly and less adaptable to recent fangles.

If I composed a personal personal, this would go between a soft spot for sunsets and an eclectic palate (hotdogs, ironically, a taste I never acquired): "abhr tpshts." After all the fuss smoothing and tucking, they constrict movement so you feel like a shrimp in an egg roll. You work all night to untangle your feet, then untangle *them* to start the pointless process all over. A clean sheet under and a quilt over is all anybody needs for year-round comfort. I sleep with one foot out (even in winter), a wick for ambient coolness to avoid sweltering in textile. With topsheets you're asking for trouble if ever a lower extremity burrows to freedom. With a comforter, easiest dance in the world: you stick your left foot out, period; makes the hokey-pokey look like a full-dress ballet. Add my redial function and the fetchingly understated ad, and this situation was ideally suited for keeping trying.

But after a day or two I'm worried this person maybe died or was abducted, because who'd run an ad if they intended being out of town? (Those who can afford nonemergency trips aren't generally famous for publicizing used bedding in the wants.) So I call the paper and ask can they verify a number, because I've kept trying for days (admitting the ad said to), and you expect a person to be home from time to time who wants to vend something. She states their sensible policy of not giving out names or addresses. I say I just want to check the number, not go and assault anybody; for all I know, the seller's this burly guy. Wait a minute, while she consults someone in a supervisory capacity (she said those actual two words). Soon I'm asking an ad manager, can we just make sure they're not misleading the numeral-reading public. Speaking in a supervisory capacity, she calls my request somewhat irregular (no kidding: "somewhat irregular"), but if I hold she'll ask her editor. Before I know it, I'm transferred to the *publisher:* would *he* double-check the phone for this comforter? You won't believe what he does. Opens up the paper and says, "Mostly blue?" I go, "That's the one." He: "Yes, that's the number we have listed." This is world-class: he checked what I'm reading, not the form the burly guy submitted! I guess nobody said you had to have any certified amount of brains to act in a publisherial capacity, and this isn't the paper of record for the entire universe, but still. I explain his error, getting him in a huff about his time is so valuable. I say I'm not asking they reveal exposé sources, I have honest fears for the personal welfare and possible life of a paying advertiser; if his time's too precious for that, maybe mine's too valuable to maintain my subscription. I slam the frank into its bun. Which is a shame, because that paper always had good variety in its wants.

By now I'm pretty heated up—this person could have a bad heart or paralysis—and considering more drastic ways to keep trying. Imagine your hotdog ringing away, and if you could only inch over and pick up, you'd get saved. This would be pure torture; I have to do something, right? But not to go off half-cocked on a false goose chase, I decide to try once more before notifying authorities, who for all I know should be dragging the lake or putting out all-pointses. Redial's shot due to calling the paper, so I punch in the number. It rings like a fire alarm. I'm about ready to get the FBI on the case when this person says, "Hello?" just like that.

Which is the absolute last thing I expected, so I say, "Are you all right?" She—it's a she—says, "Who is this calling, please?" Grasping that from her end this may sound like some crank event, I explain I've been keeping trying and almost started worrying (I omit paraplegia and drowning with cinderblocks tied to burly ankles; no point in alarming her now that she's responding to calls again). She thanks me in this sandpapery tone for my concern. I say I'm glad she's okay, because I enjoyed her wording. Right away I heard myself sounding like some smooth operator, so I just shut up, and so did she.

That got us nowhere in a big rush, you can imagine. After a minute I say, "Regarding the comforter, is it still available?" Yes; what would I like to know about it? I think, What can you know about a comforter without touching it? but that could sound like I want an unadvertised special, which I'm careful about with female vendors. So I ask things you get in ads I hate: How big, what fabric, how used (since it's all-cotton, the more the better within reason), and this totally idiotic question: "Please be more specific than mostly blue" (when it was the mostly blue, along with the keep trying, that attracted me!). Frankly, while relieved to find her alive and capacitated, I was also disappointed; now this useless sequence was embalmed in my memory till the next call, which is always the problem with getting your wish, just like in fairy tales. Regardless, she calms down, since I'm being so predictable, and *she* says, "Would you like to look at it?" which has to include touching, so she didn't take anything personally or amiss. I love this about the wants: entering homes to view goods, gleaning ideas for optimizing finite space or décor. We make a date, not for a couple days (which goes along with being out a lot). She lives on West Beverly, and says to buzz 12-A; she'll come down and admit me. You can't fault her for that; even in small cities these days it's an excellent precaution (in case your interested party is also a mass sociopath or petty thief) to take a peek before unlocking anything.

To dress, or not to dress, in mostly blue? Not that this dominates your existence for two whole days. Now and again, in the shower, bussing home from work with groceries, it slides in, like a skater working on compulsory figures while you're in freestyle mode; you intersect an infinity sign from time to time and realize something more deliberate and concerted is going on in the same rink.

Mostly blue is easy. All blue would be noticeably aforethought, but denims make you half blue already, and a cornflower T-shirt under plaid flannel does the trick without undue ostentation. In cases like this, I look for a difference to split, like driving the middle lane on a parkway: if anything comes up, you can move left or right.

I'm ready to go, and it's pouring (as Dad used to say) like Noah's buddy's business. Now what? I settle on a hat-jacket combo (umbrella's a bit much for the outfit, and with a slicker there's no turning back if a front passes rapidly). This hat features a wavy brim, so a few drops won't hurt. (Another virtue of wants and sales: track records of standing up to elements, versus new duds that can get wrecked by a single instance of weather.)

The bus is a while coming, plexiglas shelter already sardined. I'm soaked. On the bus, everybody smells like wet newsprint. Halfway, I think the sky wants to clear; hard to say with tinted windows. Debussing, I see how wishful my thinking was. Still four blocks to West Beverly, and it's coming down in slanty pails. I'm lamenting umbrella and slicker both. What if I want the comforter? That kind of article can gain some draggly weight in climate like this.

Nothing's working out as envisioned. I know my frustrations are tiny spuds on a world scale, but it puts a damper on. I'd like to go home and shower (funny, how you want that when you're ratty from the wet), but I made a date, maybe kept her from some alternative. Phones aren't the only place where you have to sometimes keep trying.

12-A (only A in the building; landlord wants the option of superstitious tenants, I guess) says: Kepler. I wonder if this comforter lady's related to the guy who figured out planetary motion is elliptical. Maybe a commoner name than I'm aware. It's the kind of buzzer where you don't hear anything; you can't be sure if you buzzed enough, but don't want to get overbearing by keeping trying. All you can do is wait. Out of the rain at least.

The elevator lacks one of those dawn-shaped indicators (I could only guess at 12-A's floor, but I'd know it was moving). Water seeps through clumped and sticky garb. But a slicker would be clammy, like I imagine skindiving, so just as well. But the wind wasn't bad, so maybe umbrella. But at this juncture that couldn't be mooter if it tried.

Dripping in a strange entryway, you can question the entire point. I mean, what if garlic powder goes stale after a time (though isn't that the point of dehydration), or who really *needs* a power sander? Still, some things—jeans or, with luck, comforters—feel so much *better* used (till a cloudburst hits and nothing feels good). So you turn your mind around again—sometimes all it takes is one thought; the outing may be worthwhile after all, like my hotdog that, if you recall, was the product of a broken home (some days you get linings out of others' clouds). I'm imagining which blues I'd favor when she wedges out of the elevator, one of these older ones with a spring-loaded expand-a-gate that I like.

Of course she hasn't got a stitch of blue on; some people just don't think that way. Wrinkly black drawstrings, a T-shirt that says something in red on purple: a bouquet of balloons with *Inflate Balloons, Not Foreign Currencies*. When she turns to shut the gate, same picture on the back, followed by *Blow Up Balloons, Not the World*. So I see she's a concerned person on a global scale. The pants go with the shirt's politics: loosely gusseted, probably organic cotton, soy-based dye. Pretty short hair (the color of dried oak leaves, if that sounded more attractive). Thongs with fat, velvety straps that, despite being orange, don't clash. Overall impression: fresh but not overly crisp, basically optimistic but nobody's fool. No tucker-in of corners, this Kepler. The lighthearted-but-not-kidding get-up fits right in with her prior wording.

I must have passed a concurrent once-over, since she admits me without shouting any questions through the door. I say, "I'm here about the comforter," immediately, to put her at ease; she goes, "Right." I drip a Hansel-Gretel trail all the way to the elevator, none too comfy inside of sopping, principally blue duds. When you get close, the gate's been painted over a few times without excessive attention to neatness. In the cage we discuss what's obvious from my moist ensemble, refraining from clichés like cats and dogs.

Turns out 12-A is third floor. Morose kidney-colored hallway, swirly apartment-house texture, quite a few layers over the years, in keeping with the elevator. Her door's heavy metal; she could have checked me out via peephole, but from the shirt I'd say she takes community responsibility seriously, won't give strangers the run of the building even if individually out of harm's way. Three or four locks, based on various principles; she does one or two, which is also like driving the middle lane (say you had to exit fast in a fire). Comforter draped over couch, and it's a beaut: none too puffy due to age, but the softest-looking thing in world history. She says I look miserable, how about something hot? Would I ever, I reply. She fills a kettle, then says maybe she can dig up dry clothes to fit. I think: Wow, you *can* tell from the wording. She brings straw-colored drawstrings, a violet sweatshirt—cornstalks, a cow grazing in front of a skyline (Chicago?)—that reads, *Smash Bi-coastal Arrogance*, alleviating any need to ask what region she hails from.

In the bathroom, a huge asparagus fern lives over the tub, where it must get its fill of humidity and frosted light. The visible toiletries are 100% natural, nothing to make you look or smell very different. Peeling off drenched denims, a peculiar chill, like a chlorinated-pool feeling, can arise. It wasn't my place to rub thighs with the only towel, and patting with t.p. didn't appeal, so I jitterbugged as an air-drying technique.

The pants are too short, which looks stupid on a man, but cozy. When I get back, something herbal is steeping. She says she'll toss my wardrobe in the basement dryer. So there I am in her (more or less) unisex duds, alone with a comforter, unspecified leaves infusing their hearts out in a bamboo egg. I resist any temptation I may have to nose around. I'm thinking when Mom urged clean undies, she meant a different kind of accident, but her point—You never know—was applicable.

She's back—her name is Gloria; by the way, mine's Fred, hi—and we're sipping jasmine (I don't say I dislike such flowery teas), approaching the mostly-blue via why she's out so much: her business is really taking off the ground (she meant taking off and getting off the ground, but I'm not sure whether she made a mistake or a little joke). I guess, on the nose (not much of a feat, given the T-shirt): one of these balloon-delivery services for birthdays and such. I ask if she dons funny costumes and recites occasional doggerel. She stiffens, like hers is a highly serious balloon enterprise; I make amends by lying about jasmine hitting the spot and surmising her job must be a pain in this weather (nodding toward ground level, though it rains just as hard at third-story altitude). She witticizes (pins nor needles nor dark of night), restoring our comfort level. I wonder, as she's out a lot, would one of those machines be useful for the business aspect. They give her the creeps (hey, me too, shuddering along inside her sweatshirt; I was just trying to make conversation). She's considered giving in to progress, though, and we collaborate briefly on greetings that obliquely reference balloon availability but remain nondescript enough for personal calls. Or, I add, unloading a comforter through the wants.

That raises the main order of business, even softer than I thought by just looking. The mostly part is tealish but cornflowery too, coordinating (she noticed) with my T-shirt. The nonmostly is mostly spring growth's yellowy green, with random berry-red splashes. Don't conclude it's a floral: these colors just swirl around (but not at all like the hallway paint job). That's lucky (especially given the suggestive tea), because I'm no fan of florals. Such personal preferences, how they arise and whether they're meaningful in a character sense, I sometimes ponder over without achieving notable success.

We're being discreet, I'll have you know, fondling diagonal corners, commenting distantly on broken-inness. I notice recent laundering, generous in line with keep trying, dryer, and jasmine (though you might ask a person's druthers, with the range of herbals on the market now). "Nice," I say, not playing hard to get as a consumer or prying as to why she'd want to rid herself. If there's a story about why, it's up to her to volunteer, and I'm not coming on strong with editorials about topsheet tangles and footwick freedom. Leaving price— always an object even if not the first issue I'd raise in a stranger's domicile.

Clad in Gloria's top and bottom, less recently washed (no expectation of company coming for them) and emanating a faint odor of what must be her, sipping *her* probably favorite tea, it's hard to bring up without feeling mercenary. She comes out and says she had fifteen or twenty in mind (conceding fifteen from the get-go, "or twenty" serving no transactional purpose but to say what she authentically had in mind). Figure the ad cost two or three; add washing, and she's not looking to make a tremendous profit here. I know I should hesitate, see how badly she wants to consummate, counteroffer ten or twelve; but fifteen (even plus busfare) seemed reasonable. Granted, fifteen isn't spare change, but recollect: this is the tenderest thing I ever ran my palms over the opposite corner of.

Maybe you don't need to know every jot of this, but I'm trying to give a sense: after alienating an entire newspaper staff, and my drowned-rat busride and all, the pleasant rhythm of this encounter mattered to me. I was monitoring my luck: changing, maybe.

Fifteen is fine, I say, if you throw in a bag to keep it dry. We hold its corners in left hands, shake with rights, square dancers on the verge of allemanding. She's got a grip, smartly up and down. In recent years, more women have learned to do this effectively; with eyes closed, you might not know which gender you're shaking with, though most folks keep theirs open when clinching deals (hers, which make contact during shaking, are—what else?—mostly blue). Her hand's less squishy than you'd guess for one who traffics in balloons, but warm as something fresh out of the dryer, where I had to wonder if my outfit, including skivvies, was still twirling and leaping like a Bolshoi dress rehearsal.

We agree to give it a few more minutes to be sure. Meanwhile, I've got this crazy thing dangling about the gusseted region of drawstrings pertaining to her. I'm concerned, what with fondling and shaking, about the prospect of displaying my own little want ad. To distract myself, I raise the topic of planetary orbits. She grins or winces (I'd know if I'd seen her do either before), and affirms somethingth somethingship, somewhat removed.

I could hardly believe my luck. Her foresomething has been a personal hero since a highly audio ninth-grade visual aid involving ball bearings and a stainless mixing bowl. Imagine owning the bedclothes of a collateral descendant of one who puzzled out something so basic and big. Underarm tufts tingled at time-sharing sweatspace with Kepler glands. Head aspin like my wash, like ball bearings, planets, I nearly dizzed out on her deep pile. My breath stepped out for some fresh air, came back in roller-coastery swoops: elliptic!

I regained balance but lost common sense, scanning for commemorative plaques: *Here Sat (Ate, Watered Her Fern) Gloria, Somewhat-removed-from Astronomically Mathematical Johannes Kepler (1571-1630)*. Was a comforter enough? I nearly put in a bid on the bi-coastal arrogance, on her teacup, her ballpoint, any relic at all of those genes.

This, remember, had been my method of prudent self-distraction from drawstrung underwearlessness. It did little to modify my dangling participle, I assure you.

I am not generally a worshipper of idols. I don't go for historical markers, celebrity house tours, viewing the shoe-horns or reading glasses of the renowned. But Kepler! I exaggerate his importance, credit him with discovering ball bearings, inventing bowls, innovating all things curvy or concave, involuted or insightful. Motions, thoughts, break-throughs. Kepler! Gosh. A man on whom I read up as a teen.

This (seeing her all-of-a-suddenly altered, elegant as a formula that plots trajectories, predictive, verifiable, robust) is hardly fair to poor Gloria, just trying to be her all-cotton, social-justice-oriented self and earn a buck cheering adults with a-candle-too-many on the cake, giving kids a bonus delight (more precious because puncture-prone) on an already special day. To her, I'm just a saturated stranger who lies about jasmine and says fifteen is fine. She's wondering if she has a plastic bag that big. But talk about special days!

Gloria proposes checking the Hotpoint. Afraid I'd be tempted, in her now venerable place, to squirrel away a bit of Kepleriana (where, in her own clothing?), I say I'll come too. "Whatever," she says, indulgent but wary, like any minute I might try something (I might, if I don't reclaim my denims soon; I'm strangely spongy in the bones). We descend, collaterally, to the cellar (stairs instead of elevator, wise on her part) in drawstrings and imperative tops: inflate, blow up, smash. From a sufficient distance, we could be twins.

The cellar room: dank, perimetrically puddled. A single forty-watter over the washer leaves other corners eerie. Metallic wet-concrete odor, like artificial sweetener in the air.

My things are done. Flannel, T-shirt, briefs (Fruit of a recent Loom, stain free, elastic intact), all fluffed up like fair-weather clouds. Jeans moist at waist and zipper where the thicknesses pile up, but, "Fine," I say, "really, fine." I start when my finger lights on a hot change-pocket rivet. Jacket's a wrinkled ball; I clutch the collar, give a whipcrack thwap: ready to wear. Not till I retrieve socks, always the last huddled afterthought out of a dryer, does it sink in: I'm barefoot on concrete. Which seems not here nor there till Gloria lowers a parking-lot-gate arm: *Stop.* There, where my step after next would have landed. She squats. Oh my, I'm thinking in the drawstrings, Gloria Kepler squatting, me watching. "Nouveau," she says, "or deco, Fred."

I try to focus past the squat. The most underrated of creatures gleams, low key, under the naked bulb: a slug. Gloria has a point; black and mauve curlicues resemble an artist's conception. Even those squishy horns waving out of what would be a head if it had one. A graceful, primitive form, plus overlaid ornamentation (with what possible adaptive value?). But then you notice the slime trail, like it sneezed and left its hankie home.

The strangest convergence: this art-appreciative close look plus quease at stepping almost *there*, a near-missed reflexive leap. Yoips, I might have said. Thank heaven not.

How it got indoors isn't the question: pedestrian, current events. The first question, we agree, being those markings. The next, we concur, being that slime. And the final, we unanimize, being our common (instinctive, universal?) reaction to both.

I actually shudder in the elevator (which, now conscious of

bare feet, I request we take), shoulders in a spasm, jiggling eye sockets, the cage for a split second wavy. Where does a creature of that magnitude come by, let alone store, such abundance of slime?

Calmer in my personal wardrobe, damp fly, hot rivets, and all, I refrain from giving hers the honest nose-to-seam sniff I might like to, fold them as if they were the freshly laundered items. A fluffy stack they make, though only two. That fern, fronding away over the tub, may be the healthiest plant I've witnessed in my life.

The comforter fills an outsized K-Mart bag. Wet hat and dry jacket laid out for my departure, like a gentleman with a valet. Wallet and keys on the coffee table. I peel ten and five from a damp wad. She presses out a smile, lifting eyebrows, awkward about the money despite being a small business-woman. "Thanks" is all I can think to say. "Really." "Thank *you*," she boomerangs, in this parody of a retailer making customers feel they got a deal (behavior after cash changes hands matters as much as anything). "I mean," I say, "for everything: tea, clothes, dryer." "Sure," she says, parodying nothing. "Even the slug," I say. We shake again, and I'm in the kidney-colored hall with my comforter. Out of curiosity, I believe I hear *two* of her several locks being utilized.

In the stairwell, half a flight down, I hear squishy steps going *snerk snerk* before I feel my warm socks wicking wetness up from the shoes.

I'm perusing the other local paper (stinks for news, but for wants is comparable; for personals, it would be a clear frontrunner). Heavy on sexual-assault and long-lost-twin-reunion fronts, snaps of folks in robes and curlers who lost everything in a blaze, photo essays on house pets of bathing beauties. This rag stops just short of reporting stories like "Theologian Asks: Adam, Eve Synthesized in Russian Lab?—

Incredible Photos Inside." I have no reason to think its staff would be more helpful in times of classified-ad distress.

This is something I've pondered: decisions we make and that make us on the basis of partial info, chance in reasoning's clothing. Take activism in a cause due to kinfolk's suffering. Say I think drunk driving is a graver problem than trash lined up improperly at curbs, but a cousin trips over a can violating a sidewalk ordinance. Complications set in, and I lose a cousin out of it. Am I likelier to agitate over curb-your-trash or driving drunk? Say I'm big in equal rights for Estonian-Americans (though I must know other groups are treated worse, this side of Estonia, anyway); one guess at my derivation. This paper thing is semi-analogous: I boycott one for deficient humanity, when for all I know this other makes them look like what Dad called The Beggar of Some-Old-Book Farm. Will I make a parallel fuss with paper #2's staff, like setting up a control group to ensure water-holding results? No; and why? If they proved just as callous, I'd be newsless, not to mention the wants. Besides, this semi-randomness—of attachments and devotions, conclusions and inconclusions—it's a lot of what life consists of, right? Especially living the way I do, as much as possible on subretail levels, you come to value serendipity.

So I'm thinking this paper decision may be dubious in the ethics area, wondering if people concerned about foreign currencies and bi-coastal arrogance are exceptions to my rule, not letting causes plop in their laps but actively seeking out maltreatments, when I happen across my favorite kind of ad in the universe. Frayman's Men's & Women's in Spinoza Park is "Going Out of Business, Everything Must Go, to Bare Walls, Per Order Bankruptcy Court." It's no gimmick; they have not only their entire inventory (what stores often mean by the abused phrase "bare walls") but—ta-daa!—"Fixtures for Sale."

I'm a fool for fixtures. Why should only retailers display

goods on merry-go-round and spiral devices, walls of chrome grid with specialized hooks? Why should the rest of us, all actual unincorporated human beings, be stuck with closets? If you like your things—and if you don't, even a great deal isn't a bargain—why not store them in plain sight? Similarly, scientific glassware: beakers, flasks, graduated cylinders—what better for decanting and table service? But where can you locate such things outside of wholesale?

Families that own department stores could, I suppose, acquire whatever they want. For the rest of us, the only way to lay hands on some items is a hen's-tooth fixtures sale. I, for example, own a lighted, revolving Timex display case (saving hours of bric-a-brac dusting) and a bent-wire drugstore bookrack (give it a twirl, and watch that complex five-o'clock shadow dance!). Such things don't appear by magic; you need to peel your eyes. Did you know mid-seventies Impala hubcaps make handsome, virtually indestructible salad bowls? (I lived on a bumpy thoroughfare, and found a dozen uses for hubcaps. A rare feeling: naked in the shower with Brillo and a sharp-edged GMC, wide as your torso, to rid of road grease. But don't get me started on hubcaps.) My point is duofold: One, you never know, not only about clean undies. Two, it pays to pay attention (because of One).

Long story short—I'm trying, you saw me back off from hubcaps, but to get a thing right, you have to sometimes be familiar with others—I give Gloria a jingle. This time I don't worry about her dying near the phone or whatnot. Still, my mustard squiggle's clammy. I say I enjoy the mostly-blue and ask her along to the Bare Walls Bargain Bash: If she *likes* fixtures, a token of gratitude for dryer and drawstrings (I omit tea, though it's the thought that counts; I'd rather not get off on the foot of lying about jasmine again).

She admits to being intrigued, but wants to get one thing straight. "A date, like?"

I say, "Not necessarily" (though her tone sounded more like necessarily not). "I think of fixtures sales," I add in a brainstorm that happens to be true, "more as an adventure."

"All right then." Since she's never been to one, she'd love to.

After hanging up, my twinkle-toe orbit loosely approximated the elliptical. How I'd characterize it is this: like I just took in a good solid dose of Gloria's helium.

Quarter past nine on the Saturday. Gloria has on black blue jeans, loose at the hips, tight at the ankles, a boatneck with red and white stripes in lieu of politics, dark glasses she removes so I needn't speculate regarding eye contact, and canvas hightops—Keds?—that remind me of childhood. She gives off this aura of health, of simply thriving.

She's a loose, creative personality, so I don't need to explain letting yourself think innovatively about in-home display strategies. I'm confident she'll see possibilities.

Frayman's so-called rock-bottom goods don't strike me as priced to fly off fixtures. I'm shocked at what they want for larger fixtures, which unfortunately are tagged (*Make an Offer*s usually go for less). Signs say: *60% Off Ticketed Price of Everything in the Store*. Asking, I'm told this reduction does not apply to fixtures. I don't fuss—it's their store, for a few more days anyway—but aren't fixtures "in the Store"? Shouldn't firms, like people, avoid saying "Everything" when they mean "everything except what you came in for"? This I found disappointing, in a store that used "bare walls" correctly.

One proof that we're not on a date is that we immediately go separate ways, she toward Misses' Sportswear, I to Men's Accessories (having already decided to get one of those feet they show socks on). I plan to check out everything, minifixtures in Infants/Toddlers to the Rubenesque racks of Women Plus. It seems seemly, though, to begin in Men's.

Frayman's has terrific feet, arched up on the balls as if

82

showing off calves (despite having no calves to speak of) and balanced off center (weighted toes are the trick). The visual aspect is charcoal grey with a splatter pattern like chuck-wagon coffeepots. Charcoal lends the foot dignity; black-&-white sprinkles add jauntiness. They make me so happy I think of getting a Boys' one, a matched set like Goldilocks ("Who's been displaying socks on *my* foot?"). But Boys' feet being pink, infinitely less elegant for living quarters, I just select a Men's, with a query or two regarding general maintenance, and are they sure they don't have the grey splatterfoot in a Boys'. I never saw sales staff so disengaged; I mean, when running a fixtures sale, should you act pissy if people want info on your fixtures? I venture as far as wondering if surly personnel helped put this store on the rocks.

Settled on my foot, I strut toward Outerwear (home of sturdy racks with hefty tags) en route to Fashion Accessories, which offers compact, often enigmatic equipment that may fall within budgetary guidelines. Clutching my splatterfoot by the ankle, I'm pleased by the outing no matter what (Gloria aside; I mean fixtureswise). One good item makes a trip worthwhile, and I plan on entering more museum mode now that I have a foot in hand. Not that I won't check prices—that'd be stupid—but I have all I need.

On my way, I spy Gloria with her first-ever fixtures—I don't believe it—a pair of stocking legs! She's tucked the ankles in her pits, legs jutting out before her; a safe way to tote such items in a crowd, maybe, but it reminds me of tank turrets. I try not to gawk.

That we both went for nether extremities, identical choices ignoring gender, pleased me. I hadn't mentioned my prior foot idea, so it was like great minds think alike (the *great* part not being the essential point of the saying). But the longer I thought, the more uncertain I got. I considered putting my foot back, which shocked me. I did put it back, then stood like an ass, dilly-dallying over this two-dollar foot. Before I could frame the issue clearly, one of my frugality maxims kicked in: *If you aren't sure you want it, you don't.*

I couldn't see what was at stake, why this should be so large a deal. Being-on-a-date? That a foot looked puny next to her legs? That the whole idea of a hosiery-display device depended on having it to myself? Some more submerged, less presentable reason? This soured me all the way from Outerwear (predictably out of my depth) to Home World (so congruous it's no fun: "Oh, wouldn't this lamp make a nice lamp?" And what they display it on is just more furniture). In Fash Acc's I run across this lucite oblong with staggered holes. I figure they showed scarves on it. It's not scratched-up. Tag's reasonable. Size is good, maybe three by four. Holes will facilitate transport. Why not, I ask, instead of why.

I'm carrying it whimsically, wrists through holes like a Puritan in the stocks, when I reunite with Gloria, who's clearly the same sort of person, content with one thing (or a matching pair). She's radiant, showing off her legs. I know that feeling, saving pleasure till you have an audience. She says fixtures are a blast (a word I haven't heard recently but it makes her point). She's so happy we came, though only being polite I think about my lucite wall. She's got dynamite legs, suggestive by virtue of balancing on tiptoes, till I notice: two right feet! At the extreme verge of pointing that out, on the idiot assumption she'd exchange one, I realize there's no reason in the world to make two versions. And B: Gloria, not compiling an authentic replica of a person up to the thighs, probably likes them identical. Close call on the think-you're-so-smart-you-say-something-stupid front.

I console myself by thinking her pinky-beige, however shapely, can't hold a candle to the splatter texture in visual-artistry terms. Another mental error: female ones are meant to show through, so splattering would be a jumbo marketing disaster, calling to mind varicosity or the heartbreak of psoriasis. I'm pondering usages of the word *sheer* when Gloria says she's not rushing me, but how about a bite when we're done here.

No expert on the neighborhood, I ask where she'd like to. "Are you done, then?" she says, and I undergo a deep inhale or two concerning the foot not taken. At this point, I'm 100%

self-conscious; if I go back for it, she'll think it's in response to her legs. (I know, so what if she did? At the time it seemed a sensible concern.) Bottom line: after covering my lucite with fidgety smudges, I resolve to let the foot go, telling myself I can come back later in case of nonbuyer's remorse. The whole situation is sheer in an unrelated sense.

"Yeah," I say, "… I'm done." In a line of people carrying such things as dozens of men's hankies, out-of-style headgear, never-in-style costume jewelry, all at 60% off, I stare at *All Sales Final*, while Gloria reviews walking-distance lunch spots.

My holes go for four dollars, 0% off. I could have two feet for this level of cash. Two right feet, yes, but undeniably a better value. Plus, the two idea grows on me, gains a foothold. I'm confused: the foot idea was mine, but two-that-match belongs to Gloria—a brilliant refinement I'd never think up (though I did have that useless Goldilocks brainstorm). I'm dying to reveal how I love the splatter pattern, ask if she'd mind my having two, explain they stop at mid-calf; would she feel weird, walking out with parallel lower extremities? But Gloria is the last person on earth I can consult with, because of the date issue: my fretting about this would highlight that. I achieve a state of moral paralysis by the time we reach the register. I let her go ahead with her legs (considerably over two dollars, I note). Then—I can't believe her flexibility, after so long in line—she says no, she won't mind if I reconsider and meet her outside. "Take your time," she says, though I know she's thinking lunchy thoughts. As she exits, swinging her limbs, a jaunty new quadruped, I strive to gather my wits about me. I feel I may start crying, something I can't recall doing in a department store since I gave Mom the slip in lingerie, thinking I was so clever, then got terrified she wouldn't want me back, when I was eight, if that.

I'm supposedly a grown man, reasonably content with my way of life. And such a fixture fan. Now it's like being bedraggled in her entryway, questioning the entire point: Who the hell needs a foot, let alone two? (If you think fetish, you're way off; feet are the least intriguing part of actual people, for my money.) What has my goat is this turmoil over what will she—with her bathtub fern, slogan shirts, squatting in cellars—think of me. What I know is, if I were her and meant what I said about not a date, I'd scurry as fast as my real legs could carry me. Because what else I know, now that she's left me alone in Frayman's, is: I want splatterfeet pretty bad, but I might want Gloria worse.

When I say *want*, I don't refer chiefly to grunting and sweating under the mostly-blue. I mean I hoped to foster a distant possibility of things going right. When you meet someone, it's like points on a checklist: interested in slugs, yes; matching legs, yes; abides erratic checkout behavior, yes; downy underside of chin, yes. Adding up to *want*, here in the midst of a failing business and the absence so far of a single thing to hold against her.

Finally I get back on the same line with the same holes and keep Gloria waiting for nothing. Handing the cashier five, I inquire about putting a small fixture on temporary hold for a potential later-in-the-day mind change. She looks like I am this blank wall you could stare at all day without learning a thing, hands me a washed-up one like I'd panhandled it off her. You can almost hear her *not* advising me to have a nice day.

Gloria, gloriously glinting under the sun in a way that reminds me we orbit it, knows this Greek place. It occurs to me she'd know things from ballooning, like cab drivers or cops: what's where, how to get there. As we walk, sunlight brings out thousands of tiny scratches on my lucite. They yield to thousands more in other directions as it moves, like it's this device for carrying as many scratches as possible from place to place. In the store it looked so clear. You know what? I don't even care. Gloria, up to her elbows in legs, is striding along with posture that makes me feel weepy, I'm so proud to be human.

If I didn't get a checkmark on the "no" side soon, I'd think the slug episode's import was: That's exactly how I'd feel, walking around with Gloria, like this fetchingly adorned thing leaving a documentary slime trail, and sooner or later she'd be bound to see it.

Over our bite, between late breakfast and early lunch, we discussed the world of commerce. I started by confessing bafflement at how bankruptcy works, and why. For example, two Frayman's ads, same paper, different pages: one for this liquidation, one for a business-as-usual white sale at another location. Shouldn't the clan pull together, pool inventory, rally round to rescue their bare walls? Instead, one blithely sells sheets at 15% off everyday retail while another goes belly-up; two branches of the same family tree.

Gloria couldn't explain that either, but called it typical. Of what? Oh, white sales, families, the whole capitalist system, if you can even call it one. I nodded, remarked how personnel seemed surly to hostile, luckily omitting my theory of employee contributions to the facility's demise. Gloria's angle made me see my snippiness about their snippiness as ultra-uncharitable. She saw these people losing their jobs. Selling off fixtures you sell off *of* must be dreadful for a duck who's lame going on dead. In this laid-off plight, you'd likely see feet as relatively frivolous to start; a series of queries could seem callous. From their shoes, on what couldn't be one of the all-time peak days, we'd appear vulturesque, so the less circling the better. And this compassion became yet another checkmark "yes" for Gloria, while making me feel even more sluggy, minus the decorative surface.

Instead of admitting to such me-centeredness, I tried to

make it part of some overall trend, anecdoting as follows: I was bagging my own the other day. A kindness, I thought, solidarity with other links in the food chain, an instance almost of volunteerism. This checker gave me a look that could wilt my lettuce if I hadn't chosen cabbage for a change. Like food shopping is my elaborate ruse to get brown paper bags free of charge.

"The unexpected throws some people," was Gloria's comment. "Or store policy may get her in trouble if you help. Or union rules? I wouldn't get upset about it."

Did I appear upset? No, no, just putting forth an example of something.

"Besides," she said, "Frayman's is different. Imagine working your final days amidst *Bare Walls* and *All Sales Final* signs. Like watching yourself die on videotape."

I thought I could maybe understand the feeling.

Our waitress (who gave legs and holes queer looks, but belied my theory of service sectors on the skids nationwide) brought moussaka, and for me a souvlaki sandwich. An early bite triggered an ingredient cascade from its grinning nether end. I lurched to save my lap from getting both decorated and slimy, switched to utensil mode, diverted attention from my mushy pita to balloons as a line of work. Like how'd she get into it, I asked.

Her partner had a dream. Gloria nurtured it into a sole proprietorship: grosses of balloons, spools of ribbon, helium tanks, a tight ad budget, and, mostly, word-of-mouth goodwill. Gradually, Have A Gas! grew to support a payroll of two. Gloria quit her job (landscaping spring to fall, snow removal in winter) and became an equal partner.

I thought retroactively: That kind of partner?

A risky business, reliant on discretionary funds and a sense that life's basically fun. Back to a payroll of one now, a solo proprietor. Her partner married, moved out of state.

Maybe not that kind of partner. A confusing word. TV cowpokes, who never heard a discouraging one on the entire range, used it for anybody, like it just meant, Hey, you.

"How are you liking the comforter?" Gloria asked out of the mostly blue.

Caught midchew, I swallowed hard before responding, "I love it. It's ..."

"That's why I sold it," she said, eyes drifting away toward kitchen or cash register.

I didn't follow ...

"It's a splendid comforter." Her eyes met mine. We could be in a movie.

"I know," I said. Then I looked around: pastry case, grill, coffee station. I recalled the phrase, *caught in the act of being themselves.* Any camera was well-hidden, which is what I grew up thinking *candid* meant. She was looking straight at her lap. Should I reach across for a hand? One held a fork, the other curled around her coffee mug like a chrome pole on a shaky bus. "It's a terrific comforter," I said, "so soft and ... beautiful."

Gloria nodded. "But too complicated for me anymore. We got it when we moved in together. Outside of the business, it's the only thing we both owned."

Partners every which way. Instead of all those guys with sidekicks, I thought of Roy and Dale, Fred and Ginger, George and Gracie.

"I'm sorry," I said, which was half-true. Or rather, all true and all false: fully sorry for Gloria's sad pain, equally unsorry to learn her ex was out of the statewide picture. Adding up to something more complicated than an exact net total of half-sorry.

Gloria took a sip of coffee, a gander at her legs. "Dessert?" she said, and also, "So, what are you planning to do with your holes?"

"Maybe. And I'm not sure. What are you doing with your

stocking legs?"

"I'm a nut for baklava," said Gloria. "Maybe, do you think, small plants?"

"I'll give the rice pudding a test drive." I pictured those thighs sprouting spider, umbrella, impatiens. I'd never have thought of that for feet. I said, "Ivy, maybe?"

"One that takes not much water, I thought. Some nonporcupineal succulent."

I'd have gone three sentences out of my way to avoid using a word like *succulent* with Gloria on a first non-date, but I could see it immediately. "A jade?"

"A pair of jades," she said, and we ordered our sweets.

I'm a fan of little trees. I prefer tiny trees in pots to giant flowers. Maybe she agreed?

Not exactly. Jades, she'd heard, symbolize longevity.

I can't see picking décor based on what some foreign culture used to think it meant instead of how it looks. But it wasn't exactly a check in the "no" column.

Over dessert, Gloria suggested we brainstorm uses for my holes. Frankly, I can't recall any of her clever ideas. All I came up with was beanbag-toss. My mind had fogged over, wondering if she'd fill her legs with soil or just seat little pots atop the thighs. I knew where she'd keep them: left and right of an old, nonworking fireplace.

After a time she noticed the lunch crowd waiting. Lots of people work Saturdays. She would consider that: others' limited lunch hours. We paid, more than I'd planned due to unforeseen dessert and coffee turning out (unlike my pita) not to be bottomless.

So: a woman with planter legs and a man with beanbag holes instead of feet waiting at the same stop for different buses. Not knowing which would come when, we began summing up right off: This was fun, Glad I came, et cetera. It seemed that if we stopped saying these things we'd go quiet till a bus showed. Vamping, musicians call it. I wanted to insert something about having her number in my phone memory; en route to *phone memory* I passed *phone bank, memory bank.* Turning, I saw what I consider the finest invention of our century, affiliated with my parent institution. I mentioned how I love them so. Gloria made a face at the electromagnetism they deplete (or generate; I wasn't on her wavelength) 'round the clock worldwide. Joking about not letting all that energy go to waste, I said I'd scoot over, be back in a sec.

I remember when you could only put money *in* vending machines. Everybody had to think ahead, Fridays especially: How much to see me through till Monday, Where's the nearest branch, and (speaking of lunch crowds), How long a line for tellers during the noon hour? What I love about these machines on every other corner is how you don't have to think. I tend to withdraw close to the minimum, for two reasons: one, frugality, which is one of my virtues; two, I get to reuse my favorite invention sooner.

This new keyless, touch-the-screen kind slows me down. It's some static-electricity force field, not requiring actual contact. I take it easy, not to mislead the machine with careless manual dexterity. By the time it rolled out my twenty and asked if I desired another transaction, a bus was squeaking to the curb. I jabbed No and spun around, but all I saw were two pink soles—table-flat through the toes, then spectacularly arched to heels cupped in midair—floating up the steps, disappearing past the folding door. After all those parting-type comments, we never said goodbye. *Sic transit* Gloria Saturday, I thought.

Waiting for mine, I thought about so many things. The point of nylons in the first place: warmth or looks, mostly? How many appliances do run twenty-four hours in our info age? (It'd take a Johannes-class mind to map interference patterns. In my life, *hardware* was bolts, dowels; *software* was nothing.)

Lavatory-fern symbolism. Partnerships, interstate commerce; liquidation, bare walls. An openness to life experience that I admire but usually fail to emulate. As my bus arrived, a pair of splatterfeet leaped up and did a little highland fling in front of my mind's eye. I couldn't decide on the spot if the point was regret or the opposite.

I rested lucite on my toes while I dug for exact change and stood for the ride. The lines on my shoes would go away with time, I hoped. Walking home, I toted the holes before me, a visibly ineffective shield, like a one-man protest against Star Wars. I paced (all that coffee) before huddling under covers to ponder how much a person can discover in a lifespan. Example: not only that any planet's orbit is an ellipse, one of whose foci is its sun's center, not only that a line joining its center with its sun's center will traverse equal areas in equal times, but also that the square of its revolution's period must remain forever proportional to the cube of its mean distance from said sun.

I tried harder than anything for the next few days to decide why I felt mostly blue.

Why did a comforter's past throw me for loop-de-loops? Gloria had no obligation to say to prospective buyers: I should warn you, in case you find me unbelievably attractive, that this quilt, despite washing, retains painful memories of cohabitation and ensuing breakup, complicated by equitable dissolution of a business partnership (and a kid or two, for all I knew). Yet here I was after the fact with all this awareness, like the kind of ad that burdens you with knowledge. I wished she hadn't said a word about why.

You assume everyone has a history, memoirs in the making; still, glimpsing where others' orbits have taken them can be a shock. These days it's unlikely anyone in double digits is virginal, but you try not to leap to opposing conclusions either. You want not to offend, for one thing. Take Gloria's squat; that I can't help taking an interest shouldn't be her problem. She can't be obliged to ask before adopting a favorable viewing posture: Might anyone in this basement take bending at hips, knees, and ankles in an unintended spirit? So instead of yelling, Hubba-hubba, or the like, you keep any delight to yourself. If later she says, Did you notice my slug-pondering squat; would you like to see it again? then you know where you stand. If not, it's your little secret, like the word that open-sesames your auto-teller. It's like why I didn't mention Kepler kinship on our visit to the Fraymen. If I find it enticing, very well and good; but that's about me, not her.

I'm aware lots of men differ on these issues. All I can say about that is, I don't.

I couldn't just call like one of her girlfriends and chat about her legs. Any follow-up would look like I had lied, not-a-date pledgewise. (Had I? That's more an essay question than true/false.) After giving up the whole idea of a foot—every time I passed the spot I'd picked out for it, I thought, You footless slug, you—I had to stay the course. But why was I footless? Not to look like a liar about dating. And why not look that way? Because I cared what Gloria thought. And why did I care what she thought?

To crystal clarify: you want, one hand, to exploit a border-line-unique situation, and the other, same token, not to mess it up. And both hands know what the other's up to.

Patience, I remember thinking, might be easier to exercise in a more engaging line of work. Sav-Mor paid me minimal wages to comparison-shop consumer buyables—fresh peaches and day-old bread to floor polish, frozen pierogies, styling mousse, six brands of pasta sauce—with a view to honing a competitive edge. I made the rounds, supermarts and selected subsuper grocers, with price-tracking checklists; same rotation weekly, which despite my fondness for repetitive orbits didn't keep me from seeing the job as dead-end.

Don't get me wrong; I was good, pencilling in house brands, noting loss leaders, bait-and-switch strategies, estimating turnover by expiration dates, getting so-called drugstores that also compete (in health-&-beauty, snack items) added to the survey. But even doing my conscientious utmost, the flexible schedule left me way too much time for cogitation.

I guess it's obvious what I was thinking: how many birds could hypothetically get clobbered by a quick career shift into the balloon-messenger field. What's called in space travel and stock markets "a slight course correction."

A different kind of guy (the suave dude who sold me my phone, say) might insert a less straightforward foot in the door. I confess to wondering how he'd go about it. Order a balloon bouquet delivered to himself? But where would this ambush get him? And why pull the wool over someone he wants to get to know? Some people think if you like a bargain, you have fewer ethics than those who favor retail; my view is the virtual opposite. In the wants, borders are less clear between commercial and personal spheres; you therefore maybe work that much harder at drawing them sharply in your mind.

The idea of delivering things, as opposed to surreptitiously monitoring markups, grew on me. The phrase *an honorable trade* kept running around my brain. I've always had decent lung power, I started thinking, forgetting helium. Balloons, I continued after remembering, symbolize many things in life you need to keep a grip on or they float off into upper reaches and pop. Like yo-yos, tampons, certain pants—they give a good name to coming with strings attached. But mostly, they make people happy: an honorable trade.

We had a storm like the day I bussed to Beverly, with added late-afternoon thunder and strobe lightning, which I pictured my discophile hotdog vendor dancing to. I lost my power (not scary, still light out). The phone survived. Not prime balloon weather, I figured: a good time to place my job-application call, with added reference to our first-impression downpour. I picked up the dog and heard my dial tone braying like a stubborn donkey.

I knew the number, already heard in my mind's ear Gloria's pleasant melody: *poo poo pee pah pee pah poo*. But some things you circle prior to diving in. I could be 110% sure by giving my fingers a stroll. Past "Balloons—Hot Air—Excursions" to "Balloons—Novelty and Toy," where I found scads of ads. Some are florists with a sideline, but the number of straight balloon enterprises in a city this size would stun you.

This world is full of subworlds you never suspect. Not just Estonian-rights lobbies. On the amateur-enthusiast level, dahlia societies, Parcheesi associations, vehicle-brand devotees; for all I know, organized bodies of fixture freaks, Kepler fan clubs. In the world of work, well just think: somebody has to do everything. Yellow-page compilers. Relish-numeral designers. Seasoning pulverizers. Slug-control experts. Foot-splatter painters. Balloon messengers. Comparison shoppers. Each with their own lore, often a specialist vocabulary. As Mom knew all too well, You never know.

So I'm boning up on issues that would concern anyone retooling for a job in the balloon community. One watershed has to be latex versus mylar (she'd go traditional, I'd guess). Some offer cake 'n' champagne with your inflatables; others, custom imprinting. Balloons Ahoy touts its "Reasonable Helium Rentals"; don't ask me what's reasonable about renting helium. Balloonytunes sings a song, Western Balloonion a telegram with each order. Ballunatics has twenty-four-hour delivery (meaning you can order a day ahead, or they knock on strangers' doors at 3 A.M.?). When I turn the page, my eyes zoom straight to Have A Gas!—a whole eighth of a page, including familiar geopolitical T-shirt logos.

I know exactly what you're thinking: I should have seen it

coming. Yes, but since when—buzzing and waiting, short hairdo, date reluctance, the word *partner*, two right legs? Since what ambiguous fact or gesture that maybe didn't even seem so at the time?

This ad was way more revealing than the others, from "Woman Owned & Operated" to "Bouquets Hand Delivered By Concerned Balloonistas Pam Parminter & Gloria Kepler." Smack in the oblong's middle, the number I already knew: "773-5654, Keep Trying."

I laid the stupid frank down on its idiotic relish buttons. The only dim thing I could think to say, even to myself, was: "Oh." Which sufficed for the time being.

I spent a minute digesting the kibosh this ad put on my career plans. Believe it or not, what I did then is lift the phone and tap in the number near my ear for the sake of the melody—*poo poo pee pah pee pah poo*—pressing the hang-up before it rang. Which I repeatedly did with some calming effect as the storm played out and light faded to dusk, left ear warm and probably magenta against slick plastic. I listened to that number in the semidark till the fridge, rumbling into action like a grizzly out of hibernation, told me the power was back. Then I stripped to clean undies, burrowed under my comforter in spite of the humidity, and curled into a ball, which I read once is good for the spine.

Gloria's sweet comforter memories gone bitter like peaches kept too long. Like that sudden corner peaches turn, Pam colored everything for me, too; harmless implications had to be dismantled, reconfigured. I went over all I'd said: could this offend, could that? Did you ever take apart a defunct appliance—a radio, wristwatch, or camera—out of curiosity? You reach a point where you don't know what came from where, how parts nest or abut. Shapes give no clue as to function. Without a schematic, you can stare at components all night and still not fathom their springs, prongs, flanges. And so with Gloria: I couldn't jigsaw a workable puzzle from fragments coming back to me in flashes, fitful starts, unfitting finishes.

At least I didn't ask in the Greek place, What was his name, this so-called partner, this tasteless jerk who left you for another woman? (I did inquire about the neat-looking guy over her mantel, and felt stupid when she said: "Picasso's *Gertrude Stein*." Should I have known even then? Can't any-body take an interest in modern art or literature?)

I'm aware this whole area is considered a turn on, at least hypothetically enticing, by many males. I was pretty sure of wanting to know Gloria on a human-being level more than any hypothetical enticement, though I'll admit getting less oblivious to how GWFs present themselves (one thing I noted: thrifty GFs and GMs enjoy the option of reducing word-counts via the economical phrase *seeks same*). So I won't deny having thoughts, but they didn't seem to be the main thing on my mind.

I told myself nothing rules out friendship. Can't you base a fondness on a variety of things, wordings to ferns, not just cellar squats? I could still dial her up on an amicable footing. No footing's more amicable than feeding someone a meal (I love that word for its reminder of hot cereal on cold mornings). After a certain amount of hem-hawing, I hit #0 and held my breath like a diver who forgot to strap on a tank.

She answered on the first ring, what Mom used to call "sitting on the phone to hatch a conversation." I got right to business without smalltalking about her legs. "I'd like to get you over here for dinner," I said in phrasing that would have benefitted from a more extended hem-haw session, so I added, "if you're free sometime."

Gloria hushed for a medium-size minute in advance of saying, "I think I ought to tell you, Fred: I'm a lesbian."

I treated that as a backcourt lob, taking my own minute to

Thrift

consider the three-tined fork it placed in my road. One—Oh, that, I know all about it from your display ad in the yellow pages—didn't sound quite right. Two and three involved pretending: to have discerned it by other means or to be ignorant. So I added a fourth prong: "That's okay, I'd like to feed you anyway." It's not like they have specialized dietary restrictions, right?

This put the fork back in her court. She kept up a tradition of pausing before saying, "If you're having people over, that'd be great. When, where, and what should I bring?"

I chose when and told her where and "just bring yourself," a dumb thing people say.

Replacing dog in bun, I believe I intended on "having people over." First I couldn't decide who, then my place seemed so small, and finally it was too late; I couldn't admit I wanted Gloria, not people, over. Eventually, I borrowed folding chairs, crammed a table with mismatched china, shopped for a half-dozen. "This stupid charade," I called it during preparations. I had to put Joni Mitchell on the 8-track to drown out that phrase.

Not till the day before, sweeping my floor while Joni wished she had a river to skate away on, had it occurred to me: Gloria might not eat everything. On the phone, thinking sardonically about homoerotic cuisine, I didn't think: she could be subomnivorous, given the overall concerned-balloonista posture (not to mention allergies, which strike without regard to politics). Due to on-the-job provisioning, I had a full fridge. Could I call to ask if onion-smothered thighs over lemony rice, parsleyed carrot medallions, and green salad suited her, without disclosing that others weren't being had over? Staring at my dustpan, I felt like giving up. That tangle of indecipherable fluff made me want to blubber. I had to sit right down on the rug for a bit before having the bright idea of calling to research what the Greeks put in their moussaka.

ROBERT CHIBKA

Big sigh of relief when the guy starts his list with ground lamb (making chicken a virtual shoo-in).

Despite things looking up menuwise, I saw myself already in really lousy faith. I'd gone out of my way to deceive: a family-valu-pak of thighs, loaner chairs, place settings for phantasms. Based on my actions, you couldn't tell this wasn't some kind of ruse. I hadn't outright lied, but in terms of candor, I might as well order ambush balloons and answer the door in the altogether.

I wanted to be friends with Gloria, not blindside her with some crusade to convert her to what I want (or what wants me). If my faith is bad, I thought, it's from honorable motives. That set off a full-scale ethical debate, with all the usual elements: means, ends, extenuations, a bunch of pointless hooked-worm wriggling.

The cooking helped. As I cut the smotherers, crying was far from my mind. Slicing onion halves, you create one paren-thetical shape in a rainbow of sizes, midway between identical and miscellaneous. This brilliant bulb's concentric layering can't be beat for instant arcs per slice. (You wonder, could garment firms adapt the form to cut patterns in ten sizes?) Readying thighs for smothering has its rewards as well. Personally, I enjoy dredging, though it masks the subtle apricotic hues of the naked thigh.

Onions wilting nicely on the range, I got to work on my salad, always the most fun. My spiffy hubcap gleamed as I hurled in waves of multicolorful ingredients for a dish called "green" (not only lettuce, bell pepper, scallion, and commas of celery, but purple cabbage, carrot parings, roasted-red-pepper laces, radish coins, tangerine smiles, sprouts, raisins, walnuts, blueberries, and cross-section cukes, which you can hardly call green). Each cut in the shape you the cook deem most apt, every tidbit adding texture and color plus taste. Tossing's sheer joy, even if you cheat by rearranging to alert a guest to smaller,

100

surprising components before digging in. Never in its life had my Impala looked so cornucopious.

Leaping to and sashaying fro between sizzly thighs and veggies, I felt like a dancer, a whole ensemble, a troupe. I'd splurged on a white not bottled in Chile and precautiously stocked jasmine. Salad snugly fridged, chicken and rice progressing, carrots at the ready. For all my back-and-forth range-to-counter boogying with knife and spatula, I hadn't drawn blood or caused a major spill. I was, literally and as they say, cooking with gas. Name me one activity that combines self-indulgence and generosity in as neat a package as special-occasion meal prep for someone you foresee appreciating the effort.

Have I mentioned my mobile? Bay window, front room: the solar system (not to scale, or Pluto'd be in another zip code), suspended so each planet rotates and revolves at the slightest ripple. This dangle-your-own-cosmos kit is one thing I picked up retail; the target market is astroscientific teens with an origami bent, but I don't regret a cent. From the kitchen I caught shifty glimpses: Pluto and Neptune, Mercury and Saturn, Jupiter and Venus, Mars and Earth floating around Sol in acute evening light. It made me think of big harmonious things, of Johannes and conic sections, simple intricacy and vice versa. I plopped Handel on the turntable (never found *Water Music* in 8-track format), and by the appointed time I felt just that balanced and reconciled myself. How reconciled? How free of illusions, how centered and comfy in the world? It didn't even discompose me to realize on the way to the door I still had on Dad's old Come 'N' Get It! barbecue apron.

The sight of Gloria was another story. My equilibrium flew out when I opened the door. It took a minute to register: a tight new perm that echoed Mom's rubber-flower-plastered bathing cap in my youth (aspiring Sigmunds who suppose this would enhance appeal, guess again). "Wow," I said. "Hi, different-looking Gloria."

She laughed. "Hi, same Fred. I just thought it was time for a change." A remark I took at precise face value, down to the third or fourth decimal place.

"Well, it suits you." First lie I ever told her, except my jasmine fib. It would have been true, too, of her dress, a velvety brown sheath revealing she foresaw a dinner party. I suddenly saw why hosts add, "Nothing fancy": not to lower menu expectations, but to head off semiformal attire. Gloria ignored what meager instructions I did give, bringing, besides herself, a jug of exotic juice combo I had the self-possession not to say Ugh at.

"Smells like heaven," she said, sniffing as a visual aid. She meant the caramelized onions I didn't notice anymore; coming in from outside, they can sort of knock you out. I'd pegged her as an onionista, so I got one thing right.

Thighs resting comfortably under a fragrant blanket in the covered skillet, needing just a warmup while carrots steamed. Time for a quick tour. Gloria liked the Timex case before I turned it on; when it lit up and revolved in delayed quarter turns, showing off knickknacks like a Miss America finalist, she adopted a rapt eye-level crouch (more rapt than me, even, despite engaging zigzag stresses on the velvet). She liked the drugstore bookrack, too. Less response than you'd expect from a Kepler to a solar system spinning in a window. "It's nice here," she summed up with an encompassing gesture.

I kept expecting her any minute to ask where were the others or what the hell was the deal with the others. All pent up, I finally just blurted: "The others aren't coming!"

"Oh?" Her eyebrows nearly shook hands with the perm. It struck me, some color enhancement had maybe been involved.

"No," I said. "It's all very complicated and unlikely, perhaps, but," (deep breath), "at the last minute, what happened," (gesture at table set for six, that prop's big moment), "first, Jim and Heather, neat people I thought you'd like, he's in Parks and Recreation and she does legal aid," (*deep* breath), "their neighbor's mother passed away, and they had to look after the kid, kids actually, two of them; then Sandy, who I think you'd like, and of course I thought they'd like you too, Sandy's a landscape architect and this top-priority project has to be faxed first thing, she's in for an all-nighter; leaving Tracy," (after making Sandy *she*, Tracy came as an absolute brainstorm, unisex but not too forced), "who called minutes ago, some bug picked up in Central America, where ..." (Stymied at the verge of a pronoun cliff, I retreated. Deepest breath of all, while thinking Chris would've done as well as Tracy.) "Tracy," I concluded, "is an anthropologist."

Whoa. Landscape architecture, mystery microbes? Heather, for Pete's sake; in my life I never met a Heather! Somehow, faced with borrowed chairs, food for a hockey team, six of everything on the table, embellishment seemed crucial. Like good money after bad. More like worse money after bad. I could have used actual friends, but none seemed as interesting as these folks. Plus, if we became friends, she might meet them, and ... it all started looking like, Oh, what a tangled web. If she'd asked what kinship any of that bore to reality, I might have confessed on the spot. Instead, she hoped everything would work out for all concerned. (*Concerned* recalling her eighth of a yellow page to my chagrin.)

Oh, I was confident it would. I'd just go put a flame under the carrots.

She adored carrots.

Good. Great. Chicken and rice, too, I hoped.

Chicken and rice with carrots sounded perfect. Mmh, the onions smelled amazing.

I uncovered the skillet with a gallant flourish, forgetting condensed steam under the lid. If not for the Come 'N' Get It!

I'd have revived a tradition of changing clothes while Gloria stood around. I managed to finish cooking without further incident. Soon we were seated, inert place settings to my left and right, her right and left.

"So where in Central America was Tracy doing this field-work?"

Oh boy. I wasn't sure. Costa Rica? (I read once they have no army.) I had a sudden image of Tracy cataloguing vivid beetles. I could shift him/her to entomology ("Did I say an*thropolo-*gist? Silly me.") or just stuff my fat mouth with chicken.

Luckily, Gloria chose that moment to compliment my smothering.

"Mmm hmm." I chewed, swallowed. "Plenty more in there," I said.

So she gathered, said Gloria, nodding at empty plates.

"I'd better make sure I turned everything off. And hey, how about a glass of wine?"

No, but she wouldn't mind some fore pee.

I had to beg her pardon.

The juice thing she brought: pineapple, pear, papaya, pome-granate. Pee pee pee pee.

"Oh, *four* pee. Absolutely. Be right back."

In the kitchen I rested elbows on counter, hyperventilated like a guy dropping out of a marathon. If only I hadn't picked that dumb name, planting traps for myself. If Tracy's male, the event seems suspiciously boy-girl-boy-girl (boy-boy-girl-girl didn't occur to me); if she's female, it looks like I stacked the deck with single women. But Tracy wasn't the problem; it was me, lying through my teeth out of such allegedly honorable motives.

The brown bag was still on the counter: Quadru-P All-Natural Organic Juice Medley. I poured a glass. Starting the wine myself was the last thing I wanted (next to last if you include Quadru-P). I filled a tumbler with water and tossed back a sizable slug.

And it couldn't be the perm. People had a right to alter hairdos. No, it was me, all topsy-turvy. Gloria, whose visual appeal easily survived an unfortunate styling choice, just wasn't very interesting to me. I add *to me* because I know interest isn't a tree falling in a forest, but a two-way street in the beholder's mind. Gloria was Gloria, every engaging or admirable quality intact. She was present and accounted for. The problem had to be me.

To make a long meal short: it's amazing, aside from a mutual interest in women more skirted around than delved into, how much two people can not have in common. Gloria, for instance, didn't give her unqualified stamp of approval to my line of work. I emphasized the consumer-advocacy aspect— an ebbing tide sinking all pricetags—but to her the job smacked of quote-unquote corporate espionage. Her refrain was Sav-Mor's evil largeness: "You serve a huge corporation," she said, as if size were everything. "Is small automatically pure, then?" I ungenerously asked. She retorted about camels navigating needles. "They treat me right," I said, "and I'm not exactly management." "Capital's dual job," she argued: "convincing labor its work is public-interested and that labor isn't maltreated to boot." Well, say Have A Gas! grew, by dint of virtue or by virtue of dint—top-notch latex, caring customer service—into a franchise operation: Have A Chain Of Gasses! Would she automatically become a means-of-production-owning sow, a wolf-in-wool? (Her diction, including *pawn* and *dupe*, had wounded me; I felt contentious.) Heavens defend her from expansion of that magnitude, she prayed. But wouldn't she be the same conscientious proprietor as ever? Can't people have an iota of doubt's benefit? "People, yes," she said; "corporate or governmental entities, no further than we can throw them."

Speaking of throwing and being thrown, don't think we

had only supermarketing differences. Connecting via bone-less thighs, I asked how she liked her plaster legs. I'd day-dreamed accurately that they framed her hearth; "They look perfectly andironic," she said, and I quote, "though I'd have preferred two that were mere images." In what light, if not that of mere images, did she view those hoseless props? "No," she objected, "mere images, mere: left and right." Gloria meant *mirror*. (By the bye: so much for red-herring same-legs clues to orientation.) Call me a regionalist bigot, but this ties *whore*-for-*horror* as my all-time runner-up pet pronuncia-tional peeve. Might as well say *nucular*, which, despite a parade of anchorpeople and presidential candidates over the years, still rubs me wrong. I don't claim this indicates a better or worse overall person; I know variant dialects lack deep moral import. The thing to note would be how free I felt, now, to remark such a foible in her, and such a petty, pettish peeve on my part.

Seeking common ground, I related my own dumb-ass on-site near-remark about her two right feet, how I saw making two kinds would be a waste. Which, don't ask me how, led us to guess where, Rome: corporate greed and the common weal.

What bothered me so much? Not that I found her uninter-esting with partnership of any sort ruled out, but that I'd found her so interesting when I ruled it in. Things I might, pre-yellow pages, have found charmingly exotic weren't. And this troubled me why? Here's all I can figure: ranking gener-osity in its broad mental sense as cardinal, I hated seeing how much of mine derived from envisioning a chance, however long-shot, of coupling.

The camel breaker got piled on over jasmine for her, spicy blackberry for me, and flute-shaped cookies neither of us by then had much appetite for. I noted how not-to-scale my astromobile was, with an implicit apology to her libeled forebear: "And the orbits are circular, of course." "Of course," she said. "It's just a cheap ornament," I explained, "not a scientific device." Gloria thought her reply would please me: "Seems accurate enough for everyday reference, Fred. As long as the orbits are circular, who can complain?"

At that moment, she reminded me of the dodo in the publisherial capacity where I initially located her wording. She didn't have a clue as to what her own forebear taught all succeeding generations (talk about public interests, common weals!). And they say acorns don't fall far from the family tree. So yes, I wound up holding ancestry against her after all. I could just about hear the dromedary vertebrae snapping.

Then Gloria turned it bactrian by looking me in the eye and injecting, "Let me guess: Pisces? One of the water signs, I'm sure of that," and trying three others before I put her out of her misery, at which point she no-kiddingly went, "Of course," Leo made total sense, must be my moon that was waterlogged. Ye gods! I thought, she imagines leading humanity to post-capitalist utopia via pre-Copernican detours? I had a vision: Gloria, a perky, permed majorette, twirling off the parade route down dead-end Ptolemy Way, the marching band of history blaring right on without her.

"Should have known," she said. Sipping, she looked pensive. "I have a history of being attractive to Leos, though I go for air signs myself." Nothing explains attractions—taste, Oedipus, even my beloved gravitation, only describe—but no way are planetary postures on delivery day the key. It pained me to hear her engage in willful stupidity.

She fingered a cookie like a mini-baton and got ready to ask something: Tracy's birthday, I irrationally feared. "You were attracted to me, weren't you, Fred?" Emphasis on *were* and *weren't*.

My visible flinch short-circuited any need for verbal response.

"And now you're not, are you?" Emphasis nowhere. She put her cookie back on the plate with the others like a visual aid that had done its job.

"It's more complicated than that." Perm or no perm, woman owned and operated or not, Gloria was still physically magnetic. Attraction galore, hormonewise. But the chemistry as opposed to biochemistry, the pop and fizz of interest, was depleted. And the only honest thing I could say was, "Way more complicated."

"'Cause I told you I'm into women," she said. "That's confusing to you."

She was telling, not asking. "Not at all," I said. "I can see being attracted to women as well as the next guy." I stopped short of calling it the least confusing thing about her. How could I tell her that what I'd stopped fantasizing about being was friends?

She offered this: "If I were interested in men, Fred ..." Emphasis, again, on *were*.

I raised a traffic-cop hand. No point in her lying; even I find other guys more attractive. I'd never say so as a host, but I was ready for her to go.

She stood and smoothed velvet over hips, leaving trails in the nap like footprints on a dewy lawn. She'd better go, she guessed. "Thanks. Dinner was great."

Recalling how I thanked her once, "for everything," I felt suddenly italicized. Wait! Now or never. "I have to tell you," I started, and, like a diver aimed off a cliff, didn't let myself stop, "I lied."

"To me? About what?" She looked more intrigued than anything else.

I stopped, in freefall toward I didn't know what body of how-deep water. My heart hit double-time, the fast busy that says nothing about the number you dialed, the whole system's overloaded. You could have taken my pulse anywhere: elbows, sphincters, nostrils. I wanted to insist on truth: that all those heavenly bodies are no more (no less!) than humungous flying rocks. Instead, I had to pick a lie to confess. The phantom guests: Jim and Heather, Sandy, Tracy? My secret plan to work for her, in pursuit of an honorable trade? That jasmine hit the spot? What I really wanted to tell, if you can believe it, was the splatterfoot saga—not even a lie, technically. But to explain that, it seemed, would take hours, days, out of both our lives.

I don't know what possessed me to make the choice. Maybe just a loss of nerve. Maybe it was the only thing I thought might be of any future use to her. "Your hair," I said. "I liked it better before, the other way."

She twinkled like a little star. "Straight, you mean?"

I hadn't thought of it that way, of course. "For what it's worth," I said, with a teensy smile, feeling like what my father called me (and got what-for from Mom for calling me) a grand total of once in his life: a complete little shit.

"Oh," she said. "Well." She tilted her head this way and that way, a little parody of primping, pretending to use me as a mirror. "To each his own." She smiled more than I had, shrugged, and waltzed out, looking what I'd call semi-jaunty.

I opened the fridge to find room for leftovers and saw the Impala, brimming with special treats. After all that care, I'd lost total track of the salad in a maze of fabrications and disappointments.

I rolled up socks for a little one-on-none beanbag toss; not the world's most engaging game, it turns out. Though fuzzy on the rules, I'm pretty sure I lost.

I ate boneless thighs for a week, salad till I couldn't stomach the withered idea of it.

It was over between me and Gloria, whatever *it* was. I felt completely disentangled, yet nowhere near sorted out. I tried compiling lists: pluses, minuses, a mental ledger. I'm good at lists, comforted by one thing after another. I had a box of jasmine with one bag missing. Most of a half-gallon of Quadru-P (I'd liken it to beanbag, in that it passes the time). A fifth, unopened, of Chateau La Quelquechose. On the nonbeverage front, things got murkier, even limiting my list to The Big Three. One, the mostly-blue, what I went after in the first place; its past isn't haunting anymore, but after living with it a while I can see it won't last forever. Two, this expanded sense of personal self-mistrust; I don't believe I'd buy a used car from me anymore if I had one to sell. Three is an image I may never lose: the compelling woman in crinkly bottom, didactic top, squatting in a rancid cellar to get close to the unexpected gastropod. I greet this picture with shivers of pleasure and pain. Plus or minus, you tell me.

Not long after polishing off the last thigh, I paid a visit to the other, unconcerned Frayman's. I took cash, prepared to haggle, and tried to explain without swamping them in details. The Fraymanites were pellucid on the topic of their fixtures not being for sale. "You have so many, all I want is two," I whined, and wound up with a scrap of paper, an address for a regional distributor. I didn't expect it to fall in my lap—I've always been willing to scan papers, make calls, pay a fair price—but letters of inquiry to wholesalers aren't my style. I'll keep my eyes open on principle and out of habit, but in fact I knew before I went that the time for acquiring feet was long past.

What I wanted anymore was nothing you can advertise, bid on, tote home on a bus. Of those, I had enough. What I wanted relates more to the problem of the lucite holes: not a thing but a function, a better way of putting what I already had to use.

And that, I told myself like an idiot, was reason enough to place the call. Because she came up with several strategies for my holes, incredibly clever ones for all I knew, over lunch when I was totally distracted by her legs. Before I could chicken, I punched in the familiar relish bits: *poo poo pee pah pee pah poo.* I was startled when she picked up and started right in talking. Still more so as it sunk in: she wasn't talking to me at or after all. Gloria woke up, smelled the coffee, saw the writing on the wall, faced facts and the music, took stock and the bull by the horns, bit the bullet, cried uncle, gave in, gave up, went out and bought the damn machine. For the business, I guessed; keeping trying, like anything else, has its limits. The message, anyway, was businesslike, of the standard "You have reached ... I can't come ... if you leave ... I'll get back" variety. It must have been cheap, because her voice sounded tinny, canned. I almost had to laugh after hanging up, thinking how I might have gone about trying to explain the nature and purpose of my call.

It's this kind of experience that can make you want to go back and reconsider the more impersonal virtues of retail. But after a while you realize: all said and done, if that's the worst thing that ever happens from paying such close attention to the wants week after week, you're still way ahead in the long run.

Brent Spencer

My sister Sheree looks on in stunned terror
as I begin my writing career.

Brent Spencer is the author of *The Lost Son* (Arcade Publishing, 1995) and *Are We Not Men?* (Arcade, 1996). He received the Wallace Stegner Fellowship at Stanford, where he was also a Jones Lecturer in Creative Writing, and the James Michener Award at the Iowa Writers Workshop, where he earned an M.F.A. His fiction and poetry have appeared in the *Atlantic Monthly*, the *American Literary Review*, the *Missouri Review*, *GQ*, and elsewhere. His most recent book, a collection of stories, was chosen as one of the best books of 1996 by the *Village Voice*.

BRENT SPENCER
Pie Night

*B*oth of us thrown out of work at the same time—
mid-December, two pre-Christmas stabs in the back. Hazard,
from Gant's Auto World (but no more), is getting the boot to
make room for a new brother-in-law. And I'm the football
coach and gym teacher at Fallon High, until tomorrow night's
school-board meeting. It sucks. It's the pits. So we lost a few
games. So we lost all of them.

We're getting loaded in the back room of Schifano's, the
wine-tasting room, which is such a joke. Soon they'll move us
out to make way for the Taster's Club, a bunch of ancient
rum-dums who think they're something special because
they've got their own stationery. But until then we're tackling
a few longnecks, slamming down some solace. The side walls
are horror-movie red. The end walls are lined with shelves
stacked full of dusty wine bottles all lying on their sides, aimed
at us like little guns. The room's only big enough for a table
and six chairs, but it's high. And up near the skylight—the
only window—is a ratty-looking stuffed goat head looking
down. Because of the bad taxidermy its lips are curled back in
a permanent sneer. It's like the thing is saying, "I'm dead and
I don't even have a body, but I'm still better off than you
losers."

We're drinking fast, we're working hard. Haz wipes his narrow face with his hand. He's still at stage one of the three stages of being fired—crazy disbelief. Two is begging. Three: nobody knows what three is yet.

He says, "It's worse for me, Randall. Don't you see? I saw it coming. I didn't just sell his cars, I did the bastard's *books*! I was the one who told him the overhead was too high, that there was too much 'water' on the lot. And then he goes and cans me! If that isn't killing the messenger, I don't know what is." There's a faint round scar at one end of Haz's mouth where somebody tried to grind a broken beer bottle into his face. It gives his mouth a turn that makes him look like he's always ridiculing something, which mostly he is.

I have another drink. "Don't worry about it. For a while it will matter a whole lot…"

"And then?"

"And then it won't."

"I'd like to off that kid," Haz says, "that brother-in-law. I'd like to push him off the edge of the known universe. What he knows about selling cars would fit under my fingernail. You don't even want to know what I'd like to do to Mr. Wynn Gant."

We're in a dark way. There's no denying it. It's winter in Nebraska, and everyone's hopes have slipped a notch. "The time is out of joint, my friend."

Just then, the manager sticks his head in the doorway and gives us the fish eye. He says, "This time you'll really have to drink up. The Club will be here any minute."

"Yeah, right," Haz says. "You and I went to high school together. Doesn't that count for something?"

"Look, ordinary people have to *pay* for using this room. And besides, you didn't give me the time of day in high school. You only hung around your football cronies."

"Sit down. Have a drink. Be a crony."

The manager thinks about it for a second and then says, "My waitress is already giving me hell. She says she won't have time to clean up in here before the members show."

"We'll clean up," I say. "We'll leave everything the way we found it."

Haz waggles his empty bottle. "So how about a farewell round?"

The manager cocks his head, says, "I don't think so," and leaves before I can persuade him and before Haz can threaten him.

Haz reaches into the down parka sitting in the chair next to him and pulls out a bottle of bourbon. "Freaking wage slave."

He takes a hit and passes the bottle to me. I say, "We're serious about our drinking tonight."

"We're serious about everything tonight, my man. That flushing sound you hear? That's your life going down the tubes."

"Oh, geez," I say, grabbing my wrist to see my watch. "I forgot. It's Pie Night." I pull on my coat and take a slug of bourbon at the same time. "I've got to get over to the house."

"Jesus, no wonder they fired you."

"It was mostly budgetary," I say. "I told you."

"Stay for another drink."

"Got to go."

"Well, when you see Gant, do me a favor and stick an ice pick in his neck."

"Sure. *No problemo.*" I look back to wave as I leave the room. In the chair next to him, the parka is slumped into itself like a dead man.

Outside, the sidewalks are thick with snow. Five inches have fallen since last night. The plows have been through, but all they did was flatten it to a high gloss. A guy on a pair of skis slides by silently. The loneliest thing I've ever seen.

I'm late for Pie Night, but I don't want to wreck the car, so

I take it slow. Impatient drivers come wag-tailing past. Let them die. I just keep chugging along.

Bad luck. The only kind I have. Is it my fault my quarterback got a blood clot in his lung, for crying out loud? I did shove the kid, a little, but I didn't punch him like his lawyer says. What? It's okay for a kid to get the crap beat out of him on the field, but it's not okay for his coach to give him a little motivation, a little boost?

And now it's Pie Night, the night we celebrate the season. Nothing to celebrate this year, though. We haven't won a single game, not really. I couldn't get a break. And now they're shutting down football for good at Fallon. I'll be remembered as the man who killed the game.

My house is all lit up, crazy squares of light spraying onto the snow-covered lawn. Something's wrong. The street should be choked with all the players' cars, but it's almost empty.

Pie Night was Gant's idea, but it isn't right. We don't deserve Pie Night. Our only win was a forfeit. The Blue Hill Bobcats' coach died and they didn't show for the game. I don't call that a win. Once or twice we came close but something always happened. We were twelve yards from the game-winning touchdown against the Hastings Tigers when our quarterback threw a pass straight into the hands of a defensive lineman. The kid was so shocked he stood there staring at the ball like it was a human head. Our ground game was no better than our air game. Against the Burwell Braves we worked the ball down to the eight-yard line when the quarterback decided to take it in. He dropped the ball, and was dropped, on the one, watching a Brave run all the way down field for a completely superfluous touchdown. But it isn't just the quarterback. We're all bad. We stink on ice. And we definitely do not deserve Pie Night.

Since retiring as coach so he could run his little empire full-time, Gant has always been the team's unofficial sponsor. It

didn't really matter that I was the coach. To him and to everyone in town, I was nothing more than Gant's flunky. His car
dealership bought the kids uniforms and equipment. His convenience store provided the coolers of Gatorade. He's a real
booster. He even calls the boys "Wynn's winners." This season,
though, it turned into a kind of joke. More than once I heard
a pissed-off fan call us "Wynn's wieners." It was embarrassing
and nothing to celebrate. Pie Night is a tradition in our town
for winners, not wieners. But Gant insisted. He called the
whole team and said we needed something to pick up our
spirits, even though we'd had the worst season in Fallon history. He said we're winners no matter what our record. He
called most of the team before he called me. How could I
refuse?

When I push through the front door of my house, Gant
comes out of the dining room, yelling, "Maestro, you finally
made it!" He has a drink in his hand. His eyes are quick and
nervous. Janey comes after him with a drink in her hand, too.

"Randall," Janey says with a little too much excitement. She
waves me in with her drink. She's wearing jeans and the silky
blouse that clings to the curves of her breasts. Her eyes are a
little red from the contacts she's not used to wearing. She
closes the door behind me with her butt and waves her hand.

"No pie boys here, Randall." Her voice is high and lilting.
She's a little drunk. When she says my name, it has a shape I
don't recognize.

"Maestro," Gant says, raising his highball, "here's to you." He
takes a quick sip, his eyes bright over the glass. I don't like the
energy I feel flowing back and forth between them.

Gant puts his arm around my shoulders and pulls me toward
him. He thinks he's still my coach and that that gives him the
right.

"Randall? Randall?" He's not sure what he wants to say. But

then it seems like he knows exactly, he's just not ready. He settles for "No pie boys, Randall. Just like Janey says." He waves his drink at the empty room. "I'm afraid your team has a bit of a morale problem."

"This wasn't a good idea. Pie Night."

He squeezes my shoulders tighter. "No, Randall. It's losing that wasn't a good idea. All that losing. You hungry, Randall? Because I have half a mind to make you eat all that." He works me around to where I can see about a dozen pies set out on the dining-room table. "Straight from my bakery," he says, "and a total waste."

I know, I want to tell him, I've eaten those pies. But I don't say anything, and Janey brings me a highball.

Gant is not handsome, but he knows how to wear clothes, and he knows how to carry himself to look taller than he is. His head is large and round, with a haze of pale blond hair, the head of a well-fed baby. He has a way of doing simple things— looking at his watch, hooking his thumb in his waistband— that makes you think they've never been done before.

Janey won't forgive me for bringing her from Stillwater, where we went to college, back to Left Nut, Nebraska, as she calls it, where we both grew up. We've been married ten years, since just after college, but I guess this is the first real crisis we've faced. She sells real estate, which is not a good business to be in at the moment. I try to make things interesting for her, try to get her to join things like the Nebras-Kats Jazz Chorale, try to take her places like the Bug Eaters' Ball. But she won't go for it.

"Things are at a sorry pass," Gant says.

"They are," Janey says. "They are that."

The highball goes down good. Janey's standing close to Gant, making me feel like the guest, like some neighbor who stopped by for a quick one. But it's Gant who wants the quick one. I can see that. The way he sidles up to her.

He says, "Tomorrow, of course, won't be any better. Not with the school-board meeting and all. I'll tell you what, though. I'll do my best to put a good face on it. I mean, I can't save your job. That's done. But at least I might be able to keep you from going down in flames."

"Thanks, Coach," I say, downing the rest of the highball. Good, like an icicle in my brain. "Thanks, Coach Weiner, you piece of—"

"Randall!" Janey moves closer to Gant now that she has an excuse. If a snake could smile, its face would look like Gant's.

"It's all right, Janey," he says. His arm goes slowly around her shoulders, drawing her in. "What you never understood, Randall, is that the little things count for oh so much. Look at the way you dress, for instance. Out-at-elbow corduroy jackets. And those worn-out running shoes! You don't know if you want to be a professor or an athlete. Which is it—jerk or jock?"

I look down at my split-topped shoes. I like them.

"I like my shoes," I say. "I prefer these shoes to some people. You, for instance."

Then Janey. "Are you just drunk, or is it something worse than that?" She's shaking. Her eyes have gone hard and bright. "You've trashed everything else in our lives. Are you just trying to make sure you don't miss anything?"

I move to the table. "Get out of my house, Gant." The pie I pick up is oozing blue from its edges and cuts. "And take your poison pies with you, or I'll redecorate that pimp suit of yours."

Gant's just smiling. These are the moments he was made for. But not Janey.

"Get out!" she says. "*You* get out! I've had enough! You can ruin your own life, but you're *not* going to ruin mine!"

Very slowly I flip the pie upside down and let it fall onto the white tablecloth. Blue spreads out from the edges like blood.

And then there are hands on me. His. Hers.

"Out!" Janey says. Her face is twisted and red, and I try to touch it.

"Perdition, catch my soul..." But then Gant grabs my arm and cranks it behind my back.

They wrestle me to the door, and before I know it, I'm outside, the door slamming behind me. And standing at the picture window, they're holding each other close like a movie

couple who've just saved their house from a maniac. They watch. They pull each other tighter. Gant leans down and kisses the top of her head, his eyes on me and on me and on me. And then he reaches out and pulls the curtain.

Will they stand there kissing each other? Then turn off the light and move up the stairs slowly, kissing the whole way, under the light falling from the fake-crystal chandelier? And then the lights going out and the house dark? Another guy would go in there like John Wayne and stop whatever might happen, but I can't help thinking this is just one more way Gant would win, one more way the rules are changing on me. I feel giddy, not sad or outraged. I walk to the middle of my snowy front lawn and yell, as loud as I can, "So it's come to this!" I laugh, watching my words sail off like smoke.

I was never much of a player back at Fallon High, but I could hold the line and I could take a hit. Janey was a cheerleader. She looked like she'd stepped right out of a hair-color commercial. A fine, fine nose. Sharp eyes. Brown hair, with lots of muscle. It was hard to concentrate on my game when I knew she was watching. I was always too scared to ask her out. There was talk that she and the coach had a thing. I've never asked her about it, and she's never told.

After graduation I followed her to OSU. I studied exercise science while she studied English. We were in the same English class. It's not that I had never read a book. My windowsill was full of supermarket paperbacks. They were mostly galactic dick contests, but I liked them better than the books they had us read in college, which were about anything but what you thought they were about.

The professor'd say, "What does Moby represent?"

I'd say, "He represents a big white fish."

He'd give me a look that said, Wouldn't you be happier back in Podunk? But I kept at it because of Janey. It didn't matter how many times I wised off or how I strutted in front of her. She couldn't care less. The only thing that turned her on was smarts. So I rolled up my sleeves and jumped headfirst into education.

I read every assignment three times. That was the rule I

made for myself. In class and out, I asked all kinds of questions.
I figured out who the smart people were and got them to
explain things to me. Whenever one of my teachers or one of
the smart kids mentioned a book, I read it, at least some of it.
That was another rule. Pretty soon there were stacks and
stacks of library books all around my apartment.

Things really connected for me one day in Shakespeare's
Tragedies, a place I never dreamed I'd turn up in all my life.
We were on *King Lear*, the part where Cinderella tells her dad
she loves him just as much as she's supposed to and not a bit
more. That does it, he goes, I'm giving my whole kingdom to
your evil stepsisters. And then, just when the stepsisters are
ragging on her about what a first-class fool she made of
herself, Cinderella turns to them and says, "I know you what
you are." It gave me the chills, reading that. I still can't really
say why. I know you what you are. When I looked up, Janey
was watching me. I know you what you are.

Books ruined me for football. After that day, Janey and I
went to classes together, ate together, slept together, argued
about books together. We were never apart. Until now, I guess.

My house is closed up tight. They might be watching me
from a crack in the curtain. Or worse, they might not. I don't
want to think about it.

Headlights and the sound of grinding gears, the headlights
too far to one side of the street and then the other. When the
pickup comes near the house, the driver stands on the brake
and cuts the wheel, sending it into a sidelong slide that stops
about five feet from where I'm standing.

The truck is a turquoise sunset, right down to the skirting,
the kind of thing that should be painted on black velvet. It's
covered with bright yellow reflectors, flanked by gleaming
aluminum running boards, and topped with a built-in tool
box. There's a hydraulic gate on the back. When the tinted
electric window rolls down, I can hear Sinatra on the radio

singing "Angel Eyes." Haz sticks his head out, grinning through his shaggy brown hair, drunk out of his mind.

"Howdy, football crony." He offers the bottle of bourbon. "Wanna come out and play? By the way, you and me just might be eighty-sixed for life from Schifano's. I hope you're okay with that."

"No way is this your truck," I say after taking a drink. He owns a big blocky van he bought at auction from the fire company. Three years running he's won the ugly-truck contest at the Cass County Fair. He likes it for the logo on the side: "HazMat." Hazardous Materials. But the police made him paint it out. Now all that's left is his nickname.

"Get in," he says. "We're going for a ride."

He drives fast through town. The streets are troughs of ice. The wheels whine. The brakes are useless. The truck won't stop at the lights, drifting slowly sideways across every intersection. Haz doesn't even notice. He's talking, talking.

"When I was a kid," he said, "we were so poor my mom would buy bruised apples and tell us the brown spots were cinnamon.

"'Mom,' I'd say, '*under* the skin?'

"'That's the way they grow them,' she'd say. 'Special.'"

We're on the edge of town now, out near the railroad tracks, the convenience store we've talked about so many times.

He pulls into the parking lot, the headlights gleaming off the darkened storefront. "You know whose place this is. You know why we're here."

Gant owns the store. We make it a point of honor never to buy anything here. Or at any of his other businesses. It helps that the store is so far out in the boonies. The fact is that nobody much goes here, not since the chains came in. He doesn't get enough business to keep his place open past 6 P.M.

Haz takes another hit of bourbon and passes it to me. "I'm feeling malicious of intent."

"When are you not?" I ask, raising the bottle.

Haz is the kind of guy who'll start a bar fight just to spark up a dull night. I say, "You're just going to make things worse."

"Can't see how that's possible."

About that he may be right.

"Be a man, Randall."

"You be a man."

The bourbon rings against the sides of the bottle as he raises it to his mouth again. He stares over the wheel at the closed convenience store. We can see the corner of the cash machine, its blinking green eye. He passes the bottle to me and rubs his hands over the heater vent.

"Why not?" he says. "Why the flimflam not?"

"Because it's illegal," I say, "that's why not." I'm not really so much against this idea as it seems. We've talked about it before. And after tonight, I figure, anything's possible. I'm just looking for a place to put it in my mind, a way I can live with it.

"Not illegal. Not really. Not if you look at it from the right perspective." He kicks his chin toward the store. "You don't think that money's insured? To them that money means nothing. To us it means food on the table, payments on the car, self-respect. Are you getting it?"

"It's the prison part I don't get. Stealing a cash machine is like robbing a bank."

"The hell! Prison's not going to happen, man. Prison's not in our cards. And even—just for the sake of argument—even if we are caught, how bad can it be? I mean, it's not like we're packing heat. It's not like we're terrorizing some teller. We'll get no more than a slap on the wrist."

"'Packing heat'? Where'd you learn to talk like that? What is it with you, Haz? You're sounding like some kind of cheap hood."

"The economy's what's come over me, man. The big dogs've

been putting it to the little dogs for too long. It's time we got back what's ours."

"That's a pretty dumb idea."

"You want to know the truth, man? The truth is I couldn't hardly make my house payments when I *was* working. You think I'm going to have a better chance now? Wake up, buddy. I'm this close to the poor farm. I figure I've got two choices." He turns his gaze on the store. "Either I get a job in a place like this or I steal that cash machine."

"That won't save you."

"Listen to you! Big talker! You're not even really out of work yet. Not technically. So if you won't do it for you, do it for me. I won't make you take any of that dirty old money. Only I can't do this alone. Show me you're my buddy. Show me you're a man."

There was a time when Haz and I did a lot more together than just drink. We used to go ice fishing, hunting. We used to test-drive expensive cars, just for the hell of it. But somewhere along the line, all that stopped. All we end up doing now is getting drunk together. It's such a shame, really. I mean, people used to think Haz was the fastest man alive. He couldn't catch but he could find the hole and run. Nobody could touch him.

The store is cinder block except for the front wall, which is all glass. Overhead, the sign reads, *Get It and Get Out.* I have to laugh. It's like permission. And what would be the harm? Haz's right about the insurance. And this town's too strapped to have much of a police force on at night.

I imagine Janey and Gant moving slowly up my staircase, the light falling and falling. "'And when I love thee not, chaos is come again.'"

"Say what?"

I pick up Haz's gloves and pull them on—brown suede with fat seams along the back of each finger. I turn my hands over.

They're not mine anymore.

"Now you're talking!" he says, backhanding my shoulder. "Besides, if the cops do show, all we have to do is run like hell. It'll be Mr. Wynn Gant who gets in trouble." He pats the dashboard. "Good thing I know where he keeps the show-room keys."

I hear a thump as Haz takes his foot off the gas. The truck moves slowly on its own across the parking lot to the curb of the narrow walkway in front of the store. We're at a little angle, so when the tires mount the curb, they do it one at a time, like a baby climbing a step, one rubbery knee after the other. When the front of the truck taps the door, there's a sharp ache of glass. We sit there a minute, the big engine throbbing.

And then he steps on the gas. The ache turns to a groan and then to a shriek as the metal frames buckle and break, jagged wings of glass falling all around us. The door pops free and attaches itself to the front of the truck. We knock over the stack of newspapers, grinding them under our wheels. We roll past the register, knocking loose the cigarette shelf overhead, packs cascading onto the hood. We catch a couple of racks fluffy with bags of pretzels and chips. We plow slowly into a display stand, two-liter pop bottles bouncing to the floor like footballs. We don't stop until we're completely inside the store.

Out of the truck now and looking around, our shoes crunching on the broken glass. All the overpriced junk lined up neatly everywhere. I can't help feeling like we've broken into the treasure room of some sick pyramid. Who wants that stuff? Chips made from a pound of salt and a cup of grease, hot dogs made of horse hair and gristle. But the truth is it does look like treasure, all the bright bags and packages.

Haz is standing near the squat beige ATM at the back wall of the store, tying heavy orange extension cords end to end.

When he's finished, he loops one end over the machine and

ties it off.

"How do you know this'll work?"

He's busy stretching his rope of cords across the store to the waiting truck. "Because I was a Boy Scout. Because I go to the movies."

He lashes the cord to the front bumper, and we climb back inside, where he guns the engine a couple times and says, "By my calculations, this should do quite nicely."

"You flunked physics."

"The first time, sure." He puts the truck in reverse and slowly backs up, glass crunching under the fat tires. We watch the orange cord snake across the floor. By the time we've backed all the way out of the store, it's taut. The ATM just stands there, its green screen blinking stupidly.

"Give it a little more gas," I say.

When he does, the cord snaps and the truck flies halfway down the parking lot until Haz stands on the brake and slaps the gearshift into park.

"Son of a duck," he says. "That sucker must be bolted to the other side of the planet."

I've learned that, when you attempt the ridiculous and fail, it doesn't wise you up, it only makes you want to try harder. I say, "Let's find a sledgehammer and a hacksaw."

"Let's just ram it," Haz says, gunning the engine.

But before we can hash out a new plan or come to our senses, someone comes strolling across the parking lot from behind the store. A cop.

"Oh boy," Haz says.

The cop takes his time, stopping halfway to gaze at the damage, at the limp extension cords snaking through the broken front window.

"We're in it now," I say.

We could run, I guess. We could swing the truck around and lay rubber, but we don't. Maybe this is the kind of thing we were hoping would happen.

"Out for a little lawbreaking tonight, are we?" the cop says, setting his right foot on the truck's running board.

"I know this looks bad," I say, trying to catch his eye. There's something familiar about him.

"Bad!" He laughs. "You got that right, buddy. Seems like I have your full attention at last."

Haz says, "Look, pal, how about you cart us off to jail and pull the curtain on this little farce?"

The cop stands there, his gaze dropping slowly toward the ground. "I will," he says, "when I'm good and ready." But he just stands there.

A long moment of silence passes. Then Haz says, "You can't arrest us, can you. You're not supposed to be here. Why else would you hide your cruiser behind a store?"

"I could be looking for speeders," he says, "scofflaws, miscreants."

"I don't think so. I think if we go back there to your car we're going to find the seat flipped back with a nice soft pillow on the headrest and maybe a box of doughnuts on the passenger seat. Am I right, officer?" He says the last word with a sneer.

"You always had a smart mouth," the cop says, "even back in school."

That's when it hits me. Not only did the cop go to Fallon High with us, he was on the team. A lost-looking kid, a bench warmer. He had a name that was too old for him—Marshall or Ellet or something—so we gave him a nickname.

"Homework!" Haz cries. That's it, that's what everyone called him.

The cop makes a face. "You didn't even remember me."

"Under the circumstances," Haz says, gesturing at the blue uniform, the gaping hole in the wall of glass, "how can you blame us?" But the cop isn't going for it. He just stands there staring at us, his face blotchy with the cold. The years have not been kind to Homework.

"Look," I say. "We aren't really planning on anything too awful here. It's just that Coach Gant—remember him?—he owns this place, and he just fired Haz's ass from his car lot. And tomorrow he's firing my ass. And we're just looking to make some kind of statement."

The cop's face has gone dark, and I think I've screwed up our chances of walking away from this. He says, "Wynn Gant owns this place?"

"Yeah."

Homework gazes at the shattered storefront and says, "I hate that guy."

I try to remember any fights between them, but there's nothing. The worst thing I can remember is that Wynn always acted as if he didn't exist. Which is enough, I guess.

"Coach never put me in the game," he says. "Not once."

Before I can stop myself, I say, "Well, you were always doing your homework on the bench."

"I was doing my homework because he never put me in!"

"I see," I say.

"You were trapped," Haz says, "boxed in."

"That's right. You stole my thought." He gazed again at the broken storefront. "You know, you're crazy to try this."

"We know!" Haz says. "Too drunk to think straight."

"Extension cords," the cop says, shaking his head. "You're going to need something a lot stronger than that."

He goes around behind the store and comes back dragging a chain big enough to raise the *Titanic*.

"Homework!" Haz yells. "You're a genius!"

In a few minutes we've chained up the ATM and attached the other end to the front of the pickup. Haz repeats his routine from before, backing the truck away from the storefront and down the parking lot. The cop waves his hands like he's directing traffic.

"You don't think this is weird?" I say to Haz.

"The guy's all right," he says as the engine whines.

When we hear the wrenching sound of metal, we think we've done it. Then the front bumper tears off, and we go scudding down the parking lot and out into the empty highway.

"Goddamn it to hell!" Haz yells, slapping the wheel. Homework stares sadly at the chain as if it's a trained dog that's let him down.

Haz drives back up to the storefront and jumps out. "Can you believe this?"

"I thought that was going to work," Homework says. "I was all set for that to work."

"Can't get a break," Haz says. "Can't get a freaking break."

Homework says, "And I really wanted to do something to hurt that guy."

"Look on the bright side," I say. "It's his truck." We look at the mangled chrome bumper lying on the asphalt like a pair of dentures. The hood's paint job is a haze of scars. "And it's his store." We look into the ragged hole of the convenience store. Loose pieces of glass are still dropping out of the window frame. Things are scattered and leaking all over the floor.

"Yeah," Haz says, "I guess the law has been thoroughly busted."

Homework says, "Why don't I give you guys a ride home?"

On the way back, Haz says, "It's remarkable what a little larceny will do for your spirits."

We talk about how it will go tomorrow, how Gant's face will fall when he sees the destroyed store, the truck parked right next to the counter, the toothless front end tapping the freezer case.

When we get to Haz's place, he says, "You fellows want to come inside? I got the titty channel."

"Nah," I say.

"We've had our fun," Homework says, pulling over and shutting off the engine.

"It *was* fun, wasn't it?" Haz says, staring thoughtfully through the windshield. "You know what? I feel better. I feel like I felt back in the old days, when we had that come-from-behind win against the Cannoneers. Remember?"

Homework says, "You ran like a rabbit."

"I did, didn't I? It's just like that. I feel like we won something."

I say, "Well, tomorrow you'll still be out of work, and I'll still be ..." I can't think how to finish.

"What the hell," Haz says, climbing out of the cruiser. "We'll always have Pie Night. Gentlemen, we must do this again sometime!" And then he's gone.

Homework and I drive through the quiet streets without saying much, the cruiser's tires moaning against the hard-packed snow. I look at all the hopeful shops and tidy houses. Another world. Once Janey and I drove to Canada, just to see what it was like. But everything was pretty much the same, except they ate their fries with vinegar, and the French for "Finger lickin' good" turned out to mean, "Fingers taste good." Now my whole life looks like a foreign country where I can't speak the language.

When he gets to my house, Homework pulls over and shuts off the engine. The warm air inside starts to cool off immediately. All my windows are dark, but I can see a glow from the kitchen. I don't feel dangerous and witty. I don't feel anything. The orchard walls are high and hard to climb. I say, "Thanks for being a straight-up guy about all this."

"Sure," he says. "We had us a time there, didn't we?"

"Yeah."

"And Haz is right—it does make you feel better."

"Yeah." But it isn't true. I don't feel better. You can turn your back on the bear, but the bear's still there.

As I climb out of the car, I say, "You know, most nights you can find Haz and me in the tasting room at Schifano's. Why don't you drop by? Let us tarnish that badge a little."

"I could do that," he says, smiling. "I will do that."

I push off the side of his cruiser as the V-8 jumps to life. I watch him glide away, leaving me there in the brittle orange air of the streetlight.

The neighborhood is locked up tight, dark and sleeping. Most of it, anyway. But I know if I try I can find some old buzzard cleaning his gun under a bare bulb in the basement. Maybe a pair of eyes staring at the TV screen, the signal gone dead long ago.

In the dark, with the snow all around, the house doesn't look like it belongs to me anymore. And if I don't find another job, I guess it won't. Nothing will. Everything is quiet, quiet. Just the dim glow from the kitchen shining from far back inside. Maybe Janey's getting herself a glass of water. Maybe she's washing the same dish over and over. She does that sometimes, when she's nervous, and once in the middle of a sound sleep. Somehow I don't think Gant is still there. Things feel too peaceful. Or at least they feel out of control in a way I understand.

I think it was this about *King Lear*. There's the sisters, their future husbands, and the king himself all trying to outdo each other with words. I love you more than this. I love you more than that. And at the key moment, the most important one, the words that come out are pure and straight and true: "I know you what you are." I think I never heard anybody talk to me so direct before.

Snow makes you think something's holding its breath, waiting for your next move, ready to blindside you when you make the wrong one. I can do things right now. Many things.

But I won't. Tomorrow's Saturday. We'll get up bright and

early, before we've had a chance to pick an attitude. I'll take
her to breakfast at the Hungry Farmer as per usual. We'll hold
our heads in our hands and try not to look each other in the
eye. People break up over this kind of thing. People kill. But
not us. Then, with our coffee cups raised, our eyes will finally
meet. This is our life. This is the way we go.

Andrea King Kelly

*Here I am at age three with my best friend.
I'm the one on the right.*

Andrea King Kelly is in the Ph.D. program in English at Florida State University where she has been the recipient of four Kingsbury Writing Fellowships, the John Mackay Shaw Academy of American Poets Award, the Phi Kapa Phi Artist Award, and the Outstanding Graduate Creative Writing Award. She is the winner of the 1992 Hemingway Prize for short fiction, and the 1997 *Writer's Digest* contemporary short story competition. She is currently working on a novel, *Wiregrass,* a short story collection, *A Summer of Women,* a poetry collection, *Red Moon,* and a collection of personal essays, *Love Me Tender.* She is poetry editor for *International Quarterly.*

ANDREA KING KELLY
Red Moon

It is the night of the lunar eclipse
and a man I am planning to love
drops dead of a heart attack,
though I won't know this
until tomorrow. Actually,
he is driving, and slumps
dead, his heart popping softly
like a bad firecracker.

My sorrel gelding is old
and has colic this night.
The book says, "Walk the horse
unceasingly; take heart
at peristaltic sounds."
We circle the lawn in perfect
syncopation; when I press my ear
to his side, his belly is tight and silent.

In the house next door
the windows are open;
my neighbors are making love.
Is there anything
more lonely than this?
Watch your heart, I whisper.
What we say aloud
ascends to Heaven.

ANDREA KING KELLY

How God orchestrates these moments:
frozen in the arc of the stable light,
a red fox plays possum,
her heart tripping in her chest;
the red horse, deciding not to die,
shifts his weight off my shoulder
as suddenly as the sky turns red
in the middle of the night.

Across town,
at a lazy intersection,
the man puts his hand to his heart.
He is puzzled by how his life
leaves him; there is nothing
of the past, and the light he sees
at the end of the tunnel
is not white, but red.

He is dreaming, instead,
of a copper fox, a sorrel horse,
a woman whose heart
he can hear
as she opens her arms
to the luminous sky
and swears, *This*
is how I will love you.

OUR FIRST POETRY OPEN
1st-, 2nd-, and 3rd-Place Winners

First-place winner: ANDREA KING KELLY
"Red Moon"
Andrea King Kelly receives $500 for her first-place poem, which begins on page 135, preceded by her profile on page 134.

Second-place winner: SUSAN RICH
"In Search of Alternative Endings"
Susan Rich lives in the Pacific Northwest. Her book The Cartographer's Tongue/Poems of the World *will be published this year by White Pine Press, New York and Snailpress, South Africa. She has poems upcoming in* DoubleTake, Many Mountains Moving, *and* Ariel: An International Review of Literature in English. *Her work has been published in* Harvard Magazine, *the* Massachusetts Review, *and* Poet Lore. *Rich has recently returned from South Africa where she was a Fulbright Fellow investigating the intersection of poetry and human rights. Currently, she is teaching private poetry classes, writing a literary-arts column for the* Eugene Weekly, *and is on the job market.*

Third-place winner: JOHN REPP
"Another New York Poem"
John Repp grew up in Vineland, New Jersey. He has worked as a retail clerk, gravedigger, egg packer, groundskeeper, storekeeper, export manager, housepainter, freelance editor and writer, and college professor. Repp is the author of Thirst Like This *(winner of the 1990 Devins Award from the University of Missouri Press) and* Things Work Out *(Palanquin Press, 1998), and editor of* How We Live Now: Contemporary Multicultural Literature *(Bedford Books, 1992). An Associate Professor of English at Edinboro University of Pennsylvania, he has also served as Visiting Writer in Residence at Carnegie Mellon University.*

We invite you to our website (www.glimmertrain.com) to see a listing of the top twenty-five winners and finalists. We thank all entrants for sending in their work.

Jiri Kajanë

*As Mrs. Selimi moved toward me with the sharp,
pointy medal, her frail hands shaking, eyes straining
beneath thick, heavy glasses, I began to question that
glorious victory. My friends, who seemed suspiciously
slower that day, received simple blue and red sashes
for second and third—no deadly pins required.*

Time Out (UK) recently called Jiri Kajanë the best Albanian author since
Ismail Kadare. Raised in Krujë, Albania, and trained in engineering at
Tiranë University, Kajanë is the author of a number of stories, including the
collection *Sa Kushtón* (*What is the Cost?*), and over a dozen one-act plays.
Kajanë's fiction has appeared in a number of U.S. journals, including
Glimmer Train Stories.

JIRI KAJANË
Some Pleasant Daydream

Translated from Albanian
by Kevin Phelan & Bill U'Ren

As usual, Leni and I sit at the Kafe Quristi, huddled around our corner table, devising in secret a plan that probably no longer needs such secrecy. Nonetheless we continue, both hunching over my writing tablet, exchanging notes back and forth in rushed scrawls, saving our voices for only the most cryptic of comments.

"The answers seem clear," Leni whispers, mindlessly drawing a tiny soccer ball on the pad.

"Yes," I mumble, glancing around the room, "all but the one."

Back at my office in the Ministry of Slogans, I still conduct even the most mundane of conversations in hushed voices and whispers. Perhaps this is because discretion is the one—and possibly the only—true lesson that my position has taught me over the years. Then again, maybe I am just resistant to even the best of changes. I've been finding it strangely difficult to shake this vigilance of secrecy—one that the rest of the country has easily shed.

"So," I mutter, "what about number seven?"

"Yes," he whispers, tugging at his hair, frustrated, "what about number seven?"

Leni has an afternoon interview for a creative clerk position at the Ministry, and the sheet we're looking at lists the ten questions he will be asked. As of yet, neither of us has even mentioned the fact that maybe this job is not something he should pursue; because we have been trying to get him a position in Slogans for so long, it now seems inappropriate to consider the fact that he's probably better off staying in his *sous chef* position at the Hotel Dajti. Obviously, the need for food in the country will continue long after the need for slogans.

But we ignore all this and instead pore over the list. As my assistant said when he discreetly handed me the sheet in an unmarked envelope, most of the questions are actually straight-forward. "Why do you want this job?" "What do you have to offer the Ministry?" "Are you loyal to your government?" One of the ten, however, seems a little more elusive. It might even qualify as a "trick" question.

I read it again, this time just to myself. "Question Seven: What would you say is your greatest fault?" For a brief moment, I forget that we are considering Leni here, and not me. Many answers come to mind. My greatest faults— certainly there are quite a few! I don't listen well. I'm slow to understand. And often, even when I do understand, I have trouble finding the correct words for an appropriate response. Back on the day my wife Ana left, moved to her sister's apartment, she turned to me and remarked, "Isn't there something that you'd like to say?" But before I could formu-late a response, before I could produce the exact words, she got frustrated, emitted a small swooshing sound from her mouth, and exited for good.

"Should I just answer the question honestly?" Leni says, nudging me.

"Interesting," I say, surprised. "I hadn't really thought of that approach." I consider this strange tactic—honesty. "So, Leni, what's your greatest fault?"

"Probably the fact that I'm pursuing a job that offers me

little, and yet requires a tremendous amount of effort and commitment in return."

"Ah, of course," I deadpan, "though it might be best if you didn't mention that to the panel."

Leni laughs, but I can see that he is getting a bit tense about the whole thing. Perhaps it's because he's wearing what he calls "the ensemble"—black shoes, clean grey pants, and a tie that I helped him with earlier in the bathroom. Or maybe it's just the time; ten o'clock now, and the interview takes place at eleven at a conference room in Durrës. Leni has arranged for his friend Faldo to give us a ride in his Skoda. With some pressure, the friend even agreed to pick us up here at the cafe.

I had originally planned to come along for moral support, but then Leni invested me with a greater responsibility. "Here's your mission," he explained. "When you get into Faldo's car, pause for a moment, rub your nose maybe a time or two, and then say to him, 'Something smells funny in here.'"

"Why?"

"A couple of weeks back, Faldo secured a day's work driving an Italian engineer down to Vlorë. After gas and whatever expenses, he was going to make nearly twenty-four thousand lira."

"Really?"

"As it turned out, he never got to deliver the engineer to his destination."

"What happened?"

"Somewhere near Butrint, south of the curves, they came upon an awful accident. A government truck had run into the horsecart of a farmer and his wife. The horse was dead, the cart flattened, and the farmer and wife left bleeding on the side of the road. The government truck was in a ditch, its axle sprung loose, standing up like a flagpole, and a couple of the soldiers were thrown onto the pavement. When Faldo came upon the scene, a small crowd had already formed. Above the frenzy, you could hear the bleeding farmer screaming in pain. It sounded like a small animal being tortured—sharp, piercing shrieks that faded all too slowly. Some of the villagers even had their hands over their ears."

"And yet they kept watching?"

"Yes, of course," Leni continued. "Two police officers arrived and waved Faldo over, explaining how they needed to requisition his car as an ambulance. The officers could only fit the bleeding wife and the two injured soldiers into their vehicle; Faldo would have to transport the dying farmer—no choice. 'But I can't,' Faldo pleaded, 'I've got to get this engineer to Vlorë!'"

"Couldn't he fit both men—the farmer and the engineer?"

"The engineer had too much luggage—five big suitcases and two or three massive crates of tools," Leni said, holding his hands out wide, embellishing a story that probably didn't need embellishing. "Before Faldo had a chance to protest, he was a mile away, one hand on the wheel, the other trying to steady the bleeding, moaning farmer. Blood everywhere," Leni added, motioning again with the hands, "all over the seats and floor and even the dashboard."

"Wait. Is this the same car that's coming to pick us up?"

"I'm getting to that part. First though—Wait, where was I?"

"Blood everywhere."

"Right. Then suddenly it all stopped—the moaning, the writhing, even the blood. The car became eerily silent. And then the smell drifted in."

"The smell of what?"

"Hard to explain. Death, was what Faldo said. Like nothing he'd ever smelled before. Kind of sour. Stagnant. Like mildew, I suppose. In the hospital parking lot, Faldo tried cleaning out the car, hoping to eliminate the smell before it had a chance to sink in. Afterwards, he raced back to the site of the accident to see if the engineer was still around, but it was too late."

"What about the farmer's wife?"

"Neither one of them made it."

"So it was all for nothing?"

"And Faldo was stuck maybe thirty, forty miles from home with a smelly taxi, no fare, and blood-stained upholstery. A total loss. Upon his return, he cleaned out the Skoda again. And then again and again. He hasn't stopped since; he's probably gone through two dozen rags and a thousand jugs of water. Every inch of the car has been wiped over a hundred times, and yet he maintains that the smell continues. Faldo drives around town with a rag over his nose to cover up the odor. Sometimes he even wears a doctor's mask, other times a wooden clothespin across his nostrils."

"You know, Leni," I say, "maybe I don't really need to go with you to this interview. After all, I've got that samovar to repair and ..."

"No," Leni says, "you've got to come. You've got a mission."

"A mission to tell Faldo that his car smells? I don't think he needs me to remind him."

"No, it's not like that. Really," Leni pleads, "you have to come."

"How bad does it smell?" I say, relenting. "I mean, truthfully?"

"That's the thing. It doesn't smell at all!"

"Leni—"

"Okay, if anything, it smells like strong cleaning solution."

"But I thought Faldo's been driving around town with a rag over his nose?"

"Yes! Somehow, he has convinced himself that the car still smells like death. He's in a panic, ready to sell it for almost nothing."

"You want me to tell him that it smells so you can buy it cheap, right?"

"Well ..."

A horn sounds out front, and Leni turns. "It's him. Don't forget your line."

"But Leni, question seven. Your greatest fault?"

Glimmer Train Stories

Hours later, I am sitting with Faldo just outside of the building where Leni's interview took place. Although Faldo's car is comfortable and air conditioned, we wait clear across the parking lot, under the hot sun, Faldo still lamenting his lost battle with that odorless smell. Feeling the onset of a heat stroke approach, I see Leni emerging from the hall doors, talking, even joking, with a woman who looks just like Priya.

Before the big changes in our country, Priya was one of the most famous women you could hope to meet. No last name, simply "Priya," and she sang at every Party function. Her voice was a dream, an uncanny range that could handle any operatic anthem, but also keep pace with the more contemporary Party songs—the snappier, shorter tunes. Priya always wore long dresses, crested in the upper left shoulder with the Party eagle, and she fashioned her hair in a special style—pinned back with the top layer sculpted into a crown. This striking image became her nationwide trademark.

Of course, it was all strategy: the Party singer obviously had to have more than just a great voice. It wouldn't do to have an overweight or unattractive singer—no matter how impressive her vocal range. Without the beautiful image alongside it, no voice could be enough. Fortunately, Priya had both.

The first time I saw her, I was still working for Hansa Splite over at the Ministry of Symbols. We went to an unveiling of a new Enver Hoxha statue at the Palace of Culture, and before the ceremony, Priya came out and sang an anthem:

> Enver, Enver, the butterfly we know
> Came from a cocoon so meek and brown
> And as the sun and moon lights flow
> Soon our cocoon became crowned

Afterwards, once the statue had been unveiled—a bronze likeness that more resembled an Italian television star than the dour, puffy-faced Hoxha—we stood at the buffet and listened while various Party officials spoke about Priya and how they would give anything to spend the night with her. I ate my plate of oysters, salmon cakes, spiced cheese, and said nothing. Later, Priya herself appeared up front, drawing everyone else away from the buffet. And as she energetically greeted each dignitary, taking their hands, kissing their cheeks, smiling throughout, I watched and packed my jacket with extra food for Ana.

"She must really love the Party," Hansa joked, amused how everyone but the two of us had converged upon the young singer. "To sing that tripe and then gush about it afterwards, it must be difficult."

"She does have a beautiful voice, though," I offered.

"Perhaps. But is sugar still sweet after it has been poured over liver?"

Hansa was right. It was hard not to picture Priya as this empty conduit rather than the singer she seemed to be. I was sure if I could have caught her eyes, I would have met with a vacant stare.

Now, years later, I'm with her in the backseat of Faldo's tainted Skoda taxi on our return drive to the capital. Priya had been a member of the interview panel that handled Leni's application to the Ministry.

"This vehicle smells unusual," she says, upon entering.

I look at Leni, who smiles. It couldn't have gone better if he had planned it—not the interview, of course—but this comment about Faldo's car coming from the lips of the former Party singer. It fits so perfectly that I glance at Leni for a moment, checking for a look that might betray this fact. But his face shows no change. Regardless, Faldo responds to Priya's frank comment with a small, squeaky groan, as if he were about to collapse. I picture him later replaying this scene in his nightmares. He'd probably been worrying over it during our long walk to his car, imagining the worst, picturing the resplendent Priya unceremoniously plugging her nose.

"It doesn't smell so bad," I offer, trying to console him, though I do raise my inflection on the word *bad* in order to avoid entirely thwarting Leni's plan.

"Thank you, Minister," Faldo responds, "but I am afraid she is right."

I can tell that Leni is beside himself with delight, even after his unsuccessful interview and our wasted day. Of course, there is the consolation that, as Priya later explains, the interview itself was inconsequential—the position had already been promised to the panel director's nephew. Actually, this may even have been a relief to Leni, knowing that he could keep his more lucrative job in the Hotel Dajti kitchen. Plus, there was the small dividend of having been freed from making any difficult decision about his future.

"It is very nice of you to offer me this ride," Priya suddenly says, "especially after all that happened—or perhaps I should say, all that did not happen—this afternoon. I am grateful. Otherwise, I would be stuck in Durrës until the morning."

"These interviews, are they how you spend your time now?" I say.

"What do you mean?" she responds, lightly smiling. The look is not blank the way I imagined, but instead more relaxed, poised. Maybe I'd been wrong about her, or perhaps some wisdom had come to her during the country's upheaval of the past years.

"For work. This—is it your living?"

"Ah, you mean since the singing is over."

I nod.

"Yes. Minister Mati has secured for me these little jobs. It varies. This week it is interviews, and next I will counsel younger female employees in certain social graces. My job description is a bit vague for this reason."

"And you like it?"

"Mati was a great fan of mine from before, and unlike the others, he stood by me when the changes came. Everyone else was quick to single me out as the Party dupe, but Mati knew that wasn't the truth."

"What is the truth?"

"I wanted to sing," she says, but not in the defensive way I expected. Her voice is relaxed, smooth. "It was very difficult to work as a singer then. Of course, the Party was the only market available. So I ask you, is it a crime to reach your goals by achieving them through what is available?"

"Maybe this interpretation is a bit subjective. But who can say," I offer noncommittally.

"I suppose," she concedes, looking out the window at the plundered wheat fields. "And yet, it is difficult for me to accept such a conclusion from the man responsible for many of the slogans I sang."

"Indirectly responsible," I say, smiling.

"And I suppose it is not your fault that the Party's anthem writers built songs around many of your Ministry's creations," she says, eyeing me.

"True," I say, conceding in return.

"Now whose interpretation is subjective?" she smiles.

For a moment, I have the vague feeling that I'm not here in this taxi of Faldo's, not sitting next to Priya, the famous and beautiful singing luminary. Instead, it feels as though I am reenacting one of my many fights with Ana. Whether it is about love, money, or ethics, I am all too quickly reminded of my ability to find fault in others concerning something that I am guilty of as well. A contradiction, Ana used to say. A hypocrite.

Yes, I am guilty. Then, for a moment, I think of Leni. How did he answer that trick question anyway? What is his greatest fault? Personally, I could've spoken for hours on the matter. For me the tougher question might be: What is your greatest virtue?

"I'll be honest with you," Priya says, suddenly moving closer. "If it were up to me, I'd be working on commercials."

"How so?" Leni says, his head popping across the front seat divider. "You mean selling chocolate bars? Smiling for the camera and taking a bite?"

"I'd rather do that kind of singing," she responds. "Sing the commercial music. You know, like Pharaoh Coffee."

"Italian commercials?" Faldo says, shifting gears.

"Of course."

Then she launches into the Pharaoh Coffee jingle, a waltz-time ditty normally spiced with bouncy electronic pianos and relentless xylophones.

> The Pharaoh is here, the Pharaoh is here
> Brought to us from Colombia's mountains
> The Pharaoh is here, the Pharaoh is here
> Beautiful as gold on the Trevi Fountains...

As she makes her way through the piece, she also sings the instrumental accompaniment in between verses, using her hands on the seat backs to keep the beat going. She is deadly serious.

"What do you think?" she says, holding her hands out to show that the song has ended.

"Magnificent," Leni exclaims.

"Yes, yes!" Faldo agrees.

"And you, Minister?" she says, dryly.

"You'll help sell thousands of them," I say.

"No, how was the singing?"

"Oh. Great, as always."

It's quiet after that, and I can feel my *great* still hanging in the air. I begin picturing the word twisting itself into something sarcastic, or at the very least self-righteous. Certainly that was not how I had intended it. I want to pull the word back in, or just say something to break the silence, somehow clarify what I had meant, but, from my years with Ana, I know that this would not be a good idea. Whenever I said the wrong thing to Ana, I always found myself getting into more trouble with each additional clarification. The more desperately I tried to talk my way out of it, the more feverish her anger grew. Of course, that was only in the later years— at first, she simply enjoyed watching me dig myself into a hole.

"But—But—," I would stumble.

"Ah, your treasured words are failing you, aren't they, Mr. Slogan?" she would laugh.

"But—," I might protest.

Sitting in the backseat with Priya, I decide that it's best to say nothing. Instead, I simply watch as she rummages through her bag, casually retrieving a small mirror in a cracked pink case. Aware that I am watching, she makes deliberate movements, tilting the mirror in all directions to get a look at her perfect hair sculpted in that signature auburn crown. I can only imagine what the mirror would reveal if pointed in my direction.

"Perhaps," Leni is saying to Faldo, "your brother could find you another Skoda."

"Yes, yes," I can hear Faldo respond, and there is another line that follows it, though it is too muffled to understand. Faldo continues holding a worn yellow scarf to his nose, protecting himself against the phantom odors, removing it only when a shift of the gear levers becomes necessary.

"Yes, of course," Leni responds, and I'm not sure if he has

understood Faldo's garbled words, or if he's simply following some sort of script concocted earlier to ensure that Faldo will sell him the car. "And how much has Bako offered you so far?"

"Mumble, mumble," Faldo responds, entirely unaware.

Priya is also unaware, now concentrating on the tube of lipstick in her right hand and the mirror in her left. I am somewhat mesmerized by this strange process of hers. The lipstick is a pale orange, and it is contained within an industrial, almost sinister-looking steel case. It glides on smooth and seemingly with little effort—one long stroke for the bottom and two short dabs for the top. This process appears far more simplistic than the struggle Ana used to endure while applying those runny and uneven tubes she bartered for in the marketplace.

Puckering her lips, Priya turns to me. "How do I look?"

"Great," I say, trying to sound as sincere as possible. And in fact, she does look great, her new lip color making her appear completely natural, only somehow slightly better.

"Thank you," she says, smiling and looking away.

As the car suddenly accelerates, Leni yells out, "Hey, what's that?"

There's a cloud of dust way up ahead, off the side of the road.

"Did you see that?" Leni says. "A car went into the ditch." Faldo doesn't respond. I can sense that his foot has nudged harder onto the gas pedal. Our speed increases, and we begin drifting into the opposite lane, as if to pass.

"An accident?" Priya asks.

"Yes, looks like it," Leni says, now almost leaning out the window to get a better view. Because of the wild coincidence, it occurs to me for just a second that maybe Leni has concocted this entire scenario. I can just picture him, days earlier, mapping out the scene, carefully rehearsing his cohorts, perhaps even drawing up some blueprints. It is an amusing vision.

"We should probably stop," I say, the cloud of dust less than two hundred meters ahead, some small red and yellow lights leaking through it.

"Yes, of course," Leni adds. Nevertheless, our speed increases.

"Oh, but Faldo, we must stop," Priya says. "Really, we must." And with that, our engine quiets and the brakes begin squeaking.

"It looks like they had a blowout and lost control!" Leni says, although I have no idea how he knows this. Only the metal hull of a small, ugly Trabant is in plain sight—light blue and rusty—peaking over a ditch.

As our car skids slightly and then stops, Leni jumps out first, then Priya. In the time that it takes me to round the car and reach the edge of the road just above the Trabant, Leni has already slid down the incline and begun surveying the damage. The car rests at a ninety-degree angle, with one side almost buried in the dirt.

"Yes! A blowout!" Leni declares, shouting to me, pointing to a spot on the car where there is in fact no wheel at all. A large part of the front end is missing, too. Some muffled yells leak from inside the car. I want to watch as Leni wipes away the dust from the only visible window, but I cannot. Instead, I allow myself to be distracted by Priya and the fluid, agile way she quickly scurries down into the ditch, not slowed at all by her fancy high-heeled shoes.

"There're people in here!" Leni yells.

"How many?" I say.

"Two," Priya declares, glancing through the dusty back window. Then she climbs around, trying to find a way in through the trunk, its meager hatch swinging in the wind.

"This thing is jammed," Leni yells, now on top of the car,

tugging at the only exposed door.

"Here, let's try to pry it open with this," Priya offers, grabbing a tire iron out of the trunk. Her crown of hair is mussed, and she appears much younger.

If these two victims really are Leni's cohorts, they're doing a great job of acting. The screams sound almost real. I grab hold and climb up top to where Leni is. As my legs kick against the hood, a hollow sound reverberates where the engine should be.

"Try this," Priya says, handing me a longer metal bar. As she does this, I catch a glimpse of Faldo, still in the driver's seat, head forward, like a horse with blinders.

On a count of three, Leni and I push down on our bars and begin prying off the door. With a crunching sound, it breaks from the car and falls into the ditch. Priya immediately reaches down and pulls out a young man from the passenger seat. He has a long gash on his head, and the blood rubs off in an equally long streak across Priya's ribcage. Leni lifts the man from her and hurriedly carries him to Faldo's car.

"Thank you, thank you," the second man mumbles as Priya helps him into my hands. He too has a similar gash right across the forehead, almost in the exact same spot.

"Panasonic," he says, looking up at me.

"What?"

"My radio. Don't leave my radio."

I look over at the dashboard, and the spot for the radio is empty, loose wires bulging through the plastic where it should be. Most of the dashboard is missing, too.

"There's nothing there," I say.

"My radio!" he says.

He continues ranting as I carry him up out of the ditch, then finally stops and takes a couple of deep breaths as I set him down. "Check the glove box," he whispers finally.

Two young kids help Leni lift the injured men into the back of Faldo's car. The small crowd that has gathered moves in closer to look at the bloody victims. Everyone stares— everyone except Faldo, whose eyes remain averted. Perhaps he is off in some pleasant daydream, although I suspect more likely it is a state of disbelief.

After they're loaded in, I go back and check the car's glove compartment. A small round transistor radio sits inside, tuned to a station full of static. I fiddle with the knobs but can't get any reception. It would have been nice to find some music for the men.

"Here," I say, handing the radio through the car window. The one man sees it and manages a smile. With both of them in the backseat, room is tight, so when she gets in, Priya is forced to sit on my lap.

"Go," Leni shouts to Faldo, jumping into the car. "The hospital's fifteen kilometers on. Hurry!"

"They're not going to die, are they?" Faldo whines from the front seat. "Please, don't die," he says to the men, glancing in the rearview mirror. "Do me that small favor, would you?"

"Hurry," Priya adds, then lightly smiles at me. It is a strange moment for levity, so perhaps it is the result of nerves.

Clutching the dirty handkerchief to his nose and mouth, Faldo quickly pulls out onto the highway towards the capital. The force of the acceleration thrusts Priya toward me; she is much lighter than I had imagined, almost weightless, and seems to merely bounce up and down on my lap. The skin on her arm feels smooth and slippery as it rubs up against my shoulder. The blood-red stains across her blouse, as well as those on my shirt, appear to have darkened.

And then for the next mile, I can hear only Leni shouting directions to Faldo above the heavy breathing of the injured men; apart from that, they remain curiously quiet and attentive, like schoolboys—as if their reaching the hospital depends upon good behavior. Out of the corner of my eye, I can see one of the two of them leaving red stains across the upholstery as he adjusts the makeshift bandage on his other arm. When we pull up to a doctor's house a few moments later— fortunately much closer than the hospital—Leni jumps out and urges Faldo to help with the injured men, leaving me and Priya alone in the empty car. And then it seems strangely quiet.

"Would you like me to get off your lap?" Priya asks, smiling. As she slides onto the seat beside me, I am suddenly struck by the incredible amount of blood all over the car. Noticing my expression, Priya also looks around.

"What a mess!" she says, nervously laughing. Again, I am surprised by this levity, and it reminds me of a wire report I'd recently read at the Ministry, something about how people respond differently in disastrous situations. During wartime, some soldiers have been known to laugh hysterically when confronted with the sight of their friends losing arms and legs and even heads. And so perhaps this is the reason, I tell myself, as Priya continues laughing even harder.

"Yes, a mess," I say, trying to calm her. Then she runs her finger through the puddle of blood beside her on the uphol- stery. For a moment, she seems almost mesmerized by the weird stains that form as she dabs it along the front seat. Seeing my perplexed look, she takes her bloodied finger, reaches over and sticks it in my mouth. Before I have time to react, the finger moves across my tongue, and I am over- whelmed by its sugary, tomato-like texture. It tastes suspiciously like the pasta sauce at the Hotel Dajti—or maybe this is my imagined version of the taste, my idea only because blood is red. What if it were brown? Would I think it tasted like chocolate? Or blue? Like berries? Priya smiles and wipes more of the fake blood across my face, "Just for looks," she says, laughing.

After a few minutes, Leni and Faldo reappear.

"Shhh," Priya says, putting the red finger across her mouth. Faldo seems almost shell-shocked as he wanders around his car, slowly examining each red stain. He circles it maybe four or five times before Leni stops him, gently putting an arm around his shoulder.

"This car is cursed!" Faldo mumbles.

It remains quiet for a few more moments until Leni breaks the silence. "Yes," he says, "I suppose it is."

"Perhaps we should go to my house," Priya suggests, "for *raki*, try to forget about this."

Faldo doesn't respond.

"Good idea," Leni finally says. "How about it, Faldo? I'll even drive."

As we make our way into town and then toward Priya's, I realize it would not surprise me to run into another wreck on the road. In fact, I almost expect it. Perhaps this one will involve two cars, maybe three, or even four. And possibly this time it might even include some women and children. But that doesn't happen. Instead, we merely pass a few goats and a horsecart full of scrap metal. The injured men and their American radio are no longer with us. We'd left them behind in the "care of the doctor," though Faldo is the only one who thinks this. Of course, mentioning it this way is not meant as an affront to Faldo; after all, the performance was concocted in his honor. Yet, somehow I can't rationalize my strange participation—or Priya's.

There are a few more questions that need to be answered. "What is your greatest fault?" At least I can help Leni out with the response for this one now. Perhaps he might answer his inability to pass up a good deal, or his inability to abstain from creating one. Regardless of how much (or little) Faldo sells his car for or how much money Leni saves on the exchange, it certainly couldn't amount to all the time and rehearsal and everything else that went into today's performance. The overturned car, the two men, Priya, even the red pasta sauce. All of it adds up. How much could Leni actually be saving? And so, perhaps the fault is more his inability to resist creating these situations, this irresistible entertainment.

Yet, if there were no victim, if Faldo weren't a dupe in the equation, certainly it would be more difficult to attribute Leni's actions to some personal fault. It is the type of caper that can make life bearable, the type of diversion that will provide enough anecdotes and stories for us to pass along for the next few months at the very least. And certainly, telling stories doesn't cost as much as everything else.

Priya's flat is not at all what I expect. It is plush, but not in the fashion of the other high-ranking officials. She does not have ornately carved wooden furniture, large Persian rugs, golden light fixtures, or garish artifacts. Instead, there are a dozen stuffed red velvet pillows across the floor, heavy beads draped over the doorways—enough to create curtains—and long sheaths of silk stretched across the walls. It is what I imagine a Bohemian smoking room might look like—or some bungalow for a turn-of-the-century spy. Ah, the comforts of Party membership!

"*Raki*, or perhaps vodka, gentlemen?" Priya says, before disappearing behind one of the beaded curtains, leaving only a clacking sound in her place. "I have some excellent types, courtesy of Minister Mati."

"Anything but Russian," Faldo says, leaning back on one of the plush floor pillows. His voice seems much calmer now, almost normal.

As Priya reenters carrying a small tray of drinks, the ice

clinking as she walks, I hear a faint tune. She's lightly humming a bouncy melody I can't place, though it's certainly not
one of the old Party numbers. As I listen to her singing and
look around the room, Leni, Faldo, and me lying down on
the floor, I have the feeling we are performing some sort of
longstanding ritual left over from a youth that I never experienced.

While we drink in silence, I begin planning the next stages
of Priya's career. It is a strange set of thoughts to have, a
strange dream—me the aging Deputy Minister as manager,
and her, the aging songstress, as a new commodity. Yes, you
may want to go into commercials, I would tell her. Certainly
they pay well. But then what? No, I envision something
completely different. Priya, I would surround you with
young male musicians, and they would have black hair and
black clothes as well. You, though, will be a blonde, with an
unusual, magnetic presence. And when people see all of you
perform, they will get the idea that they are watching much
more than an average ensemble. This would be something
new.

"Where do you get such ideas?" Priya says, pulling the
bed covers up over her shoulders. It is now hours later and,
without discussion, without decision, or even a single
clumsy moment between us, we are in her bedroom, alone.
She turns toward me and gives me a slight kiss on the cheek.
Her bed, like the rest of the flat, is silky and puffy plush, but
it also has a more classical feel to it. Perhaps this is the
canopy.

Priya twists under the covers and takes my hands.

"So you are going to help me, then? Help with my career?"
she says, but not in a way as if she's expecting an answer. This
is fortunate because it is essentially an interview question that
I would have trouble with. Can I help with her career? Will we
be together? Who can say?

I get up and head into the kitchen for a glass of water and the leftover bread from our dinner. Leni and Faldo are now asleep on the couches in the sitting room, the keys to Faldo's car and an empty vodka container on the table between them. A smile rests on Leni's face, as if in his dreams he is replaying their earlier negotiations.

"Faldo, I would love to do you a favor, but—," he had begun.

"Ah, Leni, no, don't change your mind!"

"Clearly, the car is cursed," Leni had responded. "How else can the events of today be explained?"

"Well...," Faldo had begun, and then silence. Nothing. Faldo's anguish slowly growing, my guilt surfacing, Priya, unaware, sliding her arm around my neck, and Leni smiling, doing absolutely nothing. Watching this absurd subterfuge unfold, I was struck with something my old boss, Hansa Splite, had taught me one night in the Ministry of Symbols, back when I was his apprentice. "The greatest deals," he had said, "are made with silence, not speech."

"Okay, Leni," Faldo mumbled, and then he spouted a price that seemed insanely low.

Leni said nothing.

"No, Leni, you can't buy his car," I said, interceding, gently trying to thwart a deal that was beginning to make me feel just a little too deceitful.

"But why?" Faldo implored.

"For the obvious reasons," I said, surprised at finding myself involved in the negotiation. They both looked at me for an answer. "The brakes, they are bad, yes? And the tires, bald—"

"Okay, you are right!" Faldo said, now seemingly on the edge of tears. After that he mumbled another price, this one almost half the previous amount.

Leni smiled. And then it was quiet again.

"Ah, you two are ganging up on this poor boy," Priya said, urging me off the couch, away from the negotiations, and into her bedroom. I tried to resist and make another attempt to thwart the sale, but then thought better of it. Just like the days with Ana: the more I said, the worse it got. Flaw number ten. I was unwittingly helping Leni drive the price down even lower. The rest of the bargaining would have to be heard from the confines of Priya's bed.

"Perhaps I will sell it to Bako instead," Faldo had said.

No answer from Leni.

"You know he is interested."

"Yes, Faldo, but he will have already heard about today's accident. He will know that your car is cursed." Leni cleared his throat after this in order to emphasize the word *cursed.*

"I suppose."

After that, the bartering went back and forth for quite a while. Perhaps it was thirty minutes later, when Priya was singing a small part of her favorite Party song from the old days, a song not-coincidentally based on one of my first ever slogans ("No River Is too Wide for a Bridge"), that I heard a great deal of laughter coming from the living room.

"No!"

"Yes!"

"No!"

From what I could tell, once Leni had bargained Faldo down to five leks and a half-bag of tomatoes, he revealed the entire ruse. Everything. He told Faldo about the smell, he told him about the fake accident, about the injured men, about me, Priya, all of it.

"But why didn't you just tell me to begin with?" Faldo finally said when the laughing had stopped. "Why not just say, 'Faldo, your car does not smell'?"

"I did! A hundred times. But you wouldn't listen!"

"But why the elaborate trick?"

"Because you were practically going to give your car to Bako. I couldn't let you do that. I figured if I went to this much trouble, then you'd have to believe me."

"Ah, quite true. I cannot argue with that."

It's difficult to remember where the conversation went from there. I became distracted by Priya. She mentioned something, I forget what, and then I said something back, she responded, I responded, and so forth. Somehow, I suppose we got involved in our own negotiations. And, though obviously not much of a haggler myself, I became so distracted by Leni's conversation in the other room, that my mind and mouth were shut off long enough with Priya to make things work in my favor. I did not think of Ana, and I did not think of the many faults that helped me destroy so easily and so quickly the one good thing that I once had.

"Priya, I have something to ask you," I say later, walking back into the bedroom carrying the water and breadloaf. "Something about Leni's interview—"

"I'm telling you, even if it had been flawless, it was all immaterial at that point anyway. The position had already been filled."

"No, no. That's not what I mean. I'm just wondering about one of the answers Leni gave you."

"Answers to what?"

"That question asking him to reveal his greatest fault. Number seven. What did he say?"

She thinks for a second, deliberately putting her hands under her chin for show, and turns toward me. "I think something about how his fault was that he'd do anything for a friend, even to the point of risking his own livelihood, health, or whatever. Something like that. Why?"

"And what did the panel conclude?"

"Well, it was agreed that we couldn't hire him unless he assured us that he had no friends, or at least no real friends.

You understand the security risk, yes?"

"Yes," I say.

The Last Pages

Lotte Burmeister was born July 18, 1920 in a little seacoast town on the Baltic, Travemuende, Germany. Her grandmother Burmeister always told her that it would be much better to have even a small store than to do manual work. This advice stuck with her and so in 1945, at the end of WW II set up shop in a 10'x14' room in her parents house. She was joined by her husband, Hans-Peter Matzen, who had just returned from the war. His family came from a merchant background going back to 1634. After the long war the people were in need of just about everything, shoelaces to candles and thread for darning and the people of Travemuende found it very worthwhile to beat a path to their rather out-of-the-way primarily residential area.

They were very successful and in 1948 moved to the main shopping street named "Vorderreihe" bordering the Trave River in Travemuende. They branched out to a vast variett of drygoods, fashionable clothing for women, etc. and Lotte travelled to the main cities of Germany to buy the latest in fashions and the best in merchandise. She was referred to as "the soul of the business and she loved it. In 1956 their sales volume expanded to such an extent that it enabled them to join the largest buying group in Europe, thus achieving lower costs and better pricing to beat the competition as well as a broadening of offerings from women's fashions, housewares and the latest kitchen utensils on different floors of their building.

By 1965 their two sons, Thomas and Christian, were old enough to take part in the growing business and afterwards opened two other department stores in other cities as well as 3 boutiques. Their main store in Travemuende was modernized and expandedand on the third floor opened a full-service restaurant overlooking the Trave River, with a view of huge Sandinavian ocean liners passing by periodically, so close as if almost within arm's reach. These mammoth ships thrilled the diners who were both off-the-street as well as customers from their own three selling floors. Lotte and Hans-Peter, as is often the European custom, lived on the very top floor, with a sunning deck and a beautiful view.

Lotte was highly successful in what usually was a man's world and sje far exceeded her grandmother's advice for "even a small business" being better than manual labor.

H.J.B.

GEORGE STOLZ

*H*ow many other kinds of weather were walking around the New York winter, hidden inside those big coats and clumsy shoes? How many other suns trying to emerge in the noisy steam-heat of parties and social events, in the falsely extended families and framed photographs of a different place called home?

He had read of a scientist who had not seen snow up close until adulthood; the white shock at the falling sight of it had instantly dismantled the private apparatus the poor scientist had constructed for imagining all types of unseen physical phenomenon.

How many other ways of waking? How many other ways of knowing what a physical stretch of distance is? How many other forms of boredom and evil? How many other ways of explaining why love dies? How many other ideas of Sunday afternoon? How many collective memories collectively blotted but not blotted out?

164

I don't know what to say about this story. I set out to tell a fairy tale or fable, wanting to try something different from my most recent work. Reading it now, I realize it's about meeting my husband when I was twenty-two, after losing my mother only a year and a half previous. Though not one object or person in the story is taken from my life, the emotional truth of this story is closer to autobiography than almost anything else I've written. The way truth snakes its way into fiction despite our mightiest efforts continues to amaze me.

JIRI KAJANË

*F*riendship is certainly an odd thing—both vital and elusive. Easy to recognize, impossible to describe.

Many years ago, hungrier and poorer than I've been before or since, I set out on a long walk. On a pathway just outside of the marketplace, I heard a small, unfamiliar voice call out my name. It took me a moment to recognize the girl, a young cousin of an old school friend I had met by chance weeks earlier on a bus ride to Durrës. Our conversation was somewhat brief, befitting that of two relative strangers, and yet even in the short time I remember being unable to conceal the despair that I'd been sinking into that morning. We said our good-byes, and I remember spending the rest of the day walking, clear across the hills, down the highway, and nearly all the way to Krujë. Walking was always a good way to take my mind off the empty apartment and unused kitchen.

Late that evening, already dark and somewhat cold outside, I remember stumbling across a small sack waiting there on my doorstep. Inside, there were several small, wrapped items—yogurt, chocolate, butter, and more! A string tied it all together, and a note, with the following recipe, rested on top.

Kurabie:

1 cup yogurt	½ cup soft butter
1 teaspoon baking soda	4 dashes vanilla
3 eggs	1 handful chocolate morsels
1⅛ cup sugar	1 kilogram flour (approx. 4 cups)

Mix baking soda with yogurt, add other pieces individually, work dough. Butter hands, then shape dough in small circles. Place on buttered pan, cover with beat eggs and then sprinkle sugar. Cook at medium heat.

166   *Glimmer Train Stories*

*M*y mother worked in a sewing factory for many years. Despite her mild manner, they made her union rep. One day, when a co-worker was about to be fired unfairly, she told the boss, "You fire her and I quit, and I'll take half the floor with me!" *Am I out of my cotton-picking mind?* she wondered. But when the boss apologized for the "mistake," she came to realize some of the power she never knew she had.

In the picture below, I'm having lunch with another strong woman, my daughter, in Haight-Ashbury. She's on the verge of womanhood, and I think I can see the strain of that knowledge in my face, the strain of wanting things to go right for her, for all of us. They never do, of course. Or they go right in completely unpredictable ways, ways that at first may look terribly wrong. Today Nora's a grown woman, completely her own person, and a writer of considerable talent. She's already harangued a couple of bosses in her time. I've learned courage from her, from my mother, and from the other women in my life, and I'm grateful for the lesson.

ANDREA KING KELLY

I have had an inordinate number of deaths in my life, which is why a good deal of my work is centered around this subject. "Red Moon" was written for a friend and colleague who died at thirty-nine of a heart attack. He was the kind of man I am sure inspired many eulogies, and would be quite pleased that this one has received such recognition. I also owe a debt of gratitude to my dear friend, Toni Whitfield, who insisted that I send some poems to this contest. I was tending my father through cancer at the time, and though Toni knew I was not producing or submitting any work, she professed that she had "an overwhelming feeling" that if I entered I would win. How much of this was precognition, and how much was her intuition that I needed to believe in my creative forces during that difficult time, I can't say. I do know that I listen to her advice keenly, and always trust her motives.

My thanks to Michael for the inspiration, Toni for her dedication, and *Glimmer Train* for their appreciation.

Andrea

ROBERT CHIBKA

I enjoy the densely diphthonged monosyllabic title. I'm pretty sure it was Amy Lowell's terrific feminist anti-war poem "Patterns" that got me thinking about how "thrift" can designate two first-glancingly opposite ends of a spectrum: rigorous, even self-denying economy ("thriftiness") and/or vigorous, even self-indulgent profusion ("thriving"). The "and," not the "or," of course, interested me.

Regarding self-indulgent profusion and self-denying economy: this story first arrived about fifty percent longer. I found the idea of so blowsily expansive a tale about frugality and disciplined desire amusing, but that's a tough length to get anyone thinking about publishing. I spent a while trimming, clause by dependent clause, phrase by prepositional phrase, article by definite article. To encourage myself to be slightly ruthless, I kept rehearsing this plot summary: "Boy meets girl, and nothing happens." I guess it's better now, though the packrat in me still longs to restore and retain every word. On a scale from lean elegance to chockablock clutter, I tend to favor the extremes: early on, I gorged on spare aphoristic prose and wrote teeny tiny scrimshaw-like stories, some shorter than this paragraph.

JANET DESAULNIERS

*I*n my notebook, I keep track of literary audience. This is the view from my seat.

Leslie Ullman | Stuart Dybek | Lee K. Abbott | Grace Paley

David Sedaris | Donald Justice | Doris Lessing | Thomas Lux

Helen Vendler | Ed Hirsch | Diem Jones | Mary Gordon

Yusef Komunyakaa | Laurie Stone | W.S. Merwin | John Frederick Nims

$\mathscr{P}$AST CONTRIBUTING AUTHORS AND ARTISTS

Issues 1 through 30 are available for eleven dollars each.

Robert A. Abel • Linsey Abrams • Steve Adams • Susan Alenick • Rosemary Altea • Julia Alvarez • A. Manette Ansay • Margaret Atwood • Kevin Bacon • Aida Baker • Brad Barkley • Kyle Ann Bates • Richard Bausch • Robert Bausch • Charles Baxter • Ann Beattie • Barbara Bechtold • Cathie Beck • Sallie Bingham • Kristen Birchett • Melanie Bishop • Corinne Demas Bliss • Valerie Block • Joan Bohorfoush • Harold Brodkey • Danit Brown • Kurt McGinnis Brown • Paul Brownfield • Judy Budnitz • Evan Burton • Michael Byers • Christine Byl • Gerard Byrne • Jack Cady • Annie Callan • Kevin Canty • Peter Carey • Brian Champeau • Mike Chasar • Carolyn Chute • George Clark • Dennis Clemmens • Robert Cohen • Evan S. Connell • Ellen Cooney • Wendy Counsil • Toi Derricotte • Tiziana di Marina • Junot Díaz • Stephen Dixon • Michael Dorris • Siobhan Dowd • Eugenie Doyle • Andre Dubus III • Wayne Dyer • Barbara Eiswerth • Mary Ellis • Susan Engberg • Lin Enger • James English • Tony Eprile • Louise Erdrich • Zoë Evamy • Nomi Eve • Edward Falco • Lisa Fetchko • Michael Frank • Pete Fromm • Daniel Gabriel • Ernest Gaines • Tess Gallagher • Louis Gallo • Kent Gardien • Ellen Gilchrist • Mary Gordon • Peter Gordon • Elizabeth Graver • Gail Greiner • John Griesemer • Paul Griner • Patricia Hampl • Christian Hansen • Elizabeth Logan Harris • Marina Harris • Erin Hart • Daniel Hayes • David Haynes • Daniel Hecht • Ursula Hegi • Amy Hempel • Andee Hochman • Alice Hoffman • Jack Holland • Noy Holland • Lucy Honig • Ann Hood • Linda Hornbuckle • David Huddle • Stewart David Ikeda • Lawson Fusao Inada • Elizabeth Inness-Brown • Andrea Jeyaveeran • Charles Johnson • Wayne Johnson • Thom Jones • Cyril Jones-Kellet • Elizabeth Judd • Jiri Kajanë • Hester Kaplan • Wayne Karlin • Thomas E. Kennedy • Jamaica Kincaid • Lily King • Maina wa Kinyatti • Carolyn Kizer • Carrie Knowles • Jake Kreilkamp • Marilyn Krysl • Frances Kuffel • Anatoly Kurchatkin • Victoria Lancelotta • Doug Lawson • Don Lee • Peter Lefcourt • Jon Leon • Doris Lessing • Debra Levy • Janice Levy • Christine Liotta • Rosina Lippi-Green • David Long • Salvatore Diego Lopez • Melissa Lowver • William Luvaas • Richard Lyons • Bruce Machart • Jeff MacNelly • R. Kevin Maler • Lee Martin • Alice Mattison • Jane McCafferty • Cammie McGovern • Eileen McGuire • Susan McInnis • Gregory McNamee • Jenny Drake McPhee • Frank Michel • Nancy Middleton • Alyce Miller • Katherine Min • Mary McGarry Morris • Mary Morrissy • Bernard Mulligan • Abdelrahman Munif • Kent Nelson • Sigrid Nunez • Joyce Carol Oates • Tim O'Brien • Vana O'Brien • Mary O'Dell • Chris Offutt • Elizabeth Oness • Karen Outen • Mary Overton • Patricia Page • Peter Parsons • Constance Pierce • Steven Polansky • Jessica Printz • Annie Proulx • Jonathan Raban • George Rabasa • Paul Rawlins • Nancy Reisman • Linda Reynolds • Anne Rice • Alberto Ríos • Roxana Robinson • Paulette Roeske • Stan Rogal • Frank Ronan • Elizabeth Rosen • Janice Rosenberg • Jane Rosenzweig • Karen Sagstetter • Kiran Kaur Saini • Libby Schmais • Natalie Schoen • Jim Schumock • Barbara Scot • Amy Selwyn • Catherine Seto • Bob Shacochis • Evelyn Sharenov • Ami Silber • Floyd Skloot • Gregory Spatz • Lara Stapleton • Barbara Stevens • William Styron • Liz Szabla • Paul Theroux • Abigail Thomas • Randolph Thomas • Joyce Thompson • Patrick Tierney • Andrew Toos • Patricia Traxler • Rob Trucks • Kathryn Trueblood • Carol Turner • Christine Turner • Kathleen Tyau • Michael Upchurch • A.J. Verdelle • Daniel Villasenor • Daniel Wallace • Ren Wanding • Mary Yukari Waters • Jamie Weisman • Lance Weller • Ed Weyhing • Joan Wickersham • Lex Williford • Gary Wilson • Terry Wolverton • Monica Wood • Christopher Woods • Celia Wren • Calvin Wright • Brennen Wysong • Jane Zwinger

Dorothy Grace Burmeister,
May 1947

Coming soon:

Let's say I'm a man, in his early sixties, vital enough.
I still walk eighteen holes with my son. Not a touch of
emphysema—what does one cigarette a day do, and only in
the years before my kids were born? No prostate trouble, a full
head of thin, grey hair. This is true. Let's say it's true.

from "In My Other Life" by Janet Belding

"I was asked to leave Hollywood."
Jesus, you could have knocked me over with a taco. You
really had to be pretty far gone to get run out of that town.

from "The Power Breakfast" by Peter Lefcourt

Nowadays, academics—especially the ones who are into
deconstruction and so forth—seem to go so far into the
intellectual, cerebral analysis of a book that they lose the sense
of what a book is, that a book is supposed to transport you,
take you out of yourself, do something to you that you cannot
analyze.

from an interview with Lynne Sharon Schwartz
by Nancy Middleton